# Sleigh Bells Ring

## ALYSON ROOT

J&M BOOKS

Published by J&M Books

483 Green Lanes, London, N13 4BS

Print ISBN: 978-1-917785-13-6

Ebook ISBN: 978-1-917785-15-0

Developmental Edit & Cover design by:

Tara Sullivan, The Write Gal Co.

www.thewritegal.com

Proofread By:

Crystal Lee Wren, COLProof

For my mum, who made Christmases unforgettably magical. Sleigh Bells included.

The Wisdom of Bug is written in British English.

# December 1st

Well, slap my ass and call me Rudolph. It's happening again. Damn it, I thought I was on to a winner this time 'round—

"Nic, Nicole, are you listening to me?"

Oops. "Of course I am."

"Then why aren't you saying anything?"

"What do you want me to say? You're dumping me—" I regard my watch dramatically. "—five minutes before we're due to leave for my parents' house."

"I told you I didn't want to go!"

"And, if memory serves, I said you didn't have to!"

"Which meant we'd be spending Christmas apart!"

"Seems that's happening, anyway!"

Our voices elevate to the point that Mrs Hardgrave is banging on our shared wall with her walking stick.

"Can you blame me? Last year was ridiculous!"

Now, I can deal with being dumped, even this close to the holly jolly season, but I cannot listen to her crap over the most precious annual tradition my family has.

"Ridiculous to you, but not to me or my family. You know, this is the only time we get to spend together."

"For four bloody weeks! Nobody wants to spend four weeks with their parents or siblings. It's not normal."

"It is for us, Steph. And it's twenty-five days, not four weeks."

"So, you're just going to let me walk away?"

Hell yes I am. "You made the decision, Steph."

"And you're not even going to fight me on it?"

"Is that what this is? Testing to see if I'd fight for you?"

"Well, do you blame me?"

Yes, I do. Steph is being outrageous. This is literally the only time of the year I see my family who live at the other end of the country. I've never pressured a partner to come with me. But then, to have the nerve to dump me because they can't cope with it. Like, just don't come! Surely a good and strong relationship should be able to survive twenty-five days apart, if that's what it comes to.

But now, after Steph, who is the seventeenth girlfriend to leave me since I sprung out of the closet twenty years ago, I'm starting to think my logic is flawed.

"I think you've done us a favour. I don't do 'tests', Steph. You either want to be with me, the way I am, Christmas with the family included, or you don't."

"I thought I didn't have to come?"

"What?" I have to physically turn around to make sure I'm still in my bedroom, because this is starting to feel surreal. Maybe it's a nightmare?

"You just said, Christmas with the family included, like if we want to be together, I have to go with you."

I honestly think I'd have a better chance of talking to Buddy the Elf about the intricacies of the universe than understanding what the chuffing hell Steph is saying. Have I missed the past ten minutes? She broke up with me, right?

"Stephanie, you just dumped me! What are you talking about?"

"I just want you to pick me," she screams.

I'd like to put this situation into context, just to help process this bizarre turn of events. Steph and I have been

3

together for eighteen months. She moved in with me six months ago. Since our first date, we've spent approximately forty nights away from each other. And that was only because I was working the graveyard shift, and Steph needed to meet a client on the other side of town, so staying at her place—before we cohabitated, obviously—was the better option.

I threw out a bunch of my furniture because she asked me to. I've put up with her arsehole of a best friend, who really is the worst. She changed my diet without consulting me, but I went along to make her happy. I've been choosing her all along.

My phone chimes with a hearty *ho, ho, ho,* telling me it's my mum. She's probably just checking in to make sure I'm on the road.

"Don't answer it, we're not done," Steph demands, and that's the last straw.

Picking up my phone and pointedly looking at her as I swipe the screen and begin to tap out my response, that I'm sure is utter gobbledygook, because I have no idea where my fingers are hitting, but that's just how the gingerbread biscuit crumbles. I'm not looking away first. The line has been drawn.

Twenty-five percent sure I've hit the send button, I drop the phone back on the bed. Steph crosses her arms and scowls.

"So that's it, huh? You've chosen?"

"What choice do you believe I was given?"

"Me or this stupid tradition with your family?"

I laugh. "See, there's the problem, Steph. That's not a choice. Because, for something to be a choice, it needs to be an option, and me picking you, or anyone over my family, is not an option. It's not even a consideration. Now, I'll expect you to be gone by the time I get home after Christmas."

I feel bad when I see her face drop, but then she opens her mouth again.

"Whatever, you're not even worth it, and your family is so fake. No one is that fucking happy. It's gross."

She storms around the room, ripping clothes from hangers, and grabbing underwear from our shared draw. I'm guessing I'm going to be down a few pairs of knickers now. Silently, I watch and listen to her huff and puff before she finally gives up trying to goad me and leaves.

Another jolly *ho, ho, ho* rings out, breaking me from my shock. Mum just sends question marks, which is fair.

Re-reading the message, I'm surprised she hasn't called the police thinking it was a hostage situation.

I sink to the bed and take a few seconds to quickly digest the last twenty minutes. I can't take more time, otherwise I'm going to be late starting my six-hour journey up North. However, before I finish packing, I know I need to take precautions. Steph has a vindictive side, and I really don't want to come home to find my clothes burned or my vinyls smashed. At least Reggie is coming with me. There will be no dog napping this year. I learned my lesson, when Jill, my fifth girlfriend, dumped me, and then swooped my old Corgi, Bella, up and ran out the door with her. It took me three hours to get her back.

Sighing, I pick up my phone and dial the only person who can help. "Tammy—"

"Again?"

Harsh. But fair. Tammy Sanderson has been my best friend for sixteen years. My colleague for ten. We became firefighters at the same time, but Tammy ended up stationed a couple of hours away, until she finally asked for a transfer when her deadbeat husband ran off with his receptionist.

"Yes, again. Can you stay at my place?"

"It was a bad one, then?"

"Oh yeah. I'm not entirely sure what the hell happened, but safe to say—"

"She's the type to cave your windows in?"

"Possibly."

"Your choice in women sucks, my friend. Like truly! I've never met anyone with such poor taste."

"Awesome, thanks for that. Anyway, you've got the key, and I need to get going."

"Alright babes, say hi to your parents, and give Liam an extra squeeze from me."

"Will do, thanks Tam, I owe you."

Throwing the last pieces of clothing into my suitcase, I hustle Reggie into the car. That dog has two speeds. Sleeping and zooming. He's a far cry from Bella, who would happily sleep through dinner, walks, and any other time of the day. Reggie runs in his sleep. It's exhausting just watching him. But he's got a snuggly face and even though his attitude is a bit dickish, I love that little fella.

With Reggie secured in the front seat on a booster Tammy bought him, I do a final mental check that I have everything. The presents for my family are safely stowed, as are my clothes. If I've missed anything, I'm sure I can buy it when I'm there.

"Okay, Reg, my old chum, ready to go?" His mouth opens, but chomps down on the seatbelt; I'll take that as a yes.

Motorways are the Grinch to my Who-ville, determined to suck away every drop of Christmas cheer I have. Why do people insist on undertaking? It's just stupid! Reggie agrees by yapping at the pillock climbing up my bumper. I physically cannot move out of the way, but try telling him that. Sodding Audi drivers.

Finally, we clear the traffic and I sigh a breath of relief when I see my turn coming up in a mile. Six hours is a long drive, especially with a rambunctious dog.

My Christmas cheer monitor ratchets up a notch or two as I inch closer to Hebden Bridge. My parents moved there when I was two. It's an idyllic Yorkshire town that has recently become quite the mecca for lesbians. Thank you, *Gentleman Jack*, for the recognition. Tourists overwhelm Mum's tea shop daily because of that TV programme.

The family home is located just outside the main town, down a cul-de-sac. It's one of those streets where everyone knows their neighbour—for better or worse. Can you imagine how hard it was to get away with anything when you had old Mrs Smith curtain twitching every fart's end?

In any case, Liam, Beth, and I got up to a *few* rowdy things in our youth. Mrs Smith had to take a break from being the number one busybody sometimes.

I pass the small park a few streets away from my parents' place. Fond memories of winters building snowmen fill my mind, making me smile. God, I love this time of year.

Our house is quite easy to spot, considering it's lit up like Santa's workshop. Dad does an admirable job of stringing up soft glow lights around the soffits. Thankfully, they've stopped cramming the front lawn with obnoxious blow-up ornaments. Their electricity bill was through the roof last year, which helped me convince them to give up the garden spectacle. The place looks so much better now, very classy.

Beth's car is already in the drive. Little shit got here before me and snagged the last parking spot. I hate leaving my Clio on the kerb. There's always some tit who uses the cul-de-sac as a turnaround and will inevitably clip my wing mirror. Bloody Steph, making me late.

Reggie has clocked onto our location and decides he needs to become a furry town crier, alerting all of Yorkshire of our arrival. At least he's clipped in, however unhappy that is currently making him. The first time I brought him home, he was only a pup. I stupidly thought it would be okay to leave him curled up on the front seat. The journey was a success until we arrived, and in a split second he turned into the Tasmanian Devil. It took me forever to corral him and safely get him inside the house. Well, not this year. I've learned my lesson.

The front door of my parents' four-bed, detached house flies open. Liam, my younger brother by three years, comes tumbling out, a big goofy smile on his face. My heart squeezes at the sight of him. Liam was twenty-two when he suffered an accident that starved his brain of oxygen, resulting in permanent damage. His body looks like a thirty-four-year-old but his behaviour, speech, reading, and writing are much younger.

Liam is the life and soul of the family, though. He never once let his accident get the better of him. He's our miracle.

"Nic, Nic, Nic." Liam always greets me this way when he's excited. Reggie is yelping, pulling at his bonds, desperate to bathe his favourite person—apart from me—in sloppy kisses.

"Reg, Christ calm down!" No chance. Liam is already at the passenger door, his face plastered to the window, nose smushed, giving Reggie and me a clear view up his nostrils.

With my overstimulated ball of fluff gnawing on the belt in an effort to get out, I give in, lean over, and unbuckle him. Liam rips the door open, catching Reggie mid-flight.

"Reggie, stop it." Liam giggles.

Leaving them to their love fest. I take the Reggie-free opportunity Liam has given me to grab all my crap from the boot. The presents will have to stay hidden until Liam is out of view. That dude is like a bloodhound when it comes to sniffing out gifts.

"Shoes off," Mum bellows through the house before I've even stepped over the threshold. Balancing like a goddamn professional ballerina, I get my shoes off and into the waiting pair of elf slippers. They have massive ears and a beard.

The scent of gingerbread wafts through from the kitchen, making my mouth water. I know there will be a plate full of them and a steaming mug of Baileys and hot chocolate waiting for me.

Dumping all my gear at the bottom of the stairs, I shuffle down the hall to the kitchen. Mum is in her usual spot in front of the oven, her Mrs Claus apron dusted with flour and god knows what else.

"Hey, Mum," I say, wrapping my arms around her, planting a kiss on her temple. "They smell divine."

Dropping the spatula, Mum whirls 'round, her rosy cheeks pulling up to her eyes as she smiles. "Nic, my love, it's so good to see you."

"You too. I've missed you guys."

"We've missed you too, sweety. Is Steph—"

"Not here, Mum." The sympathetic look doesn't help, but I know it's coming from a place of love. At one point, a few years back, Mum said I could skip the tradition if I wanted. I think she's worried I'm going to die alone, even though I'm not even forty yet. The idea was so preposterous, I just sat and stared at her until she rolled her eyes and mumbled, "Never mind, I'll go make some eggnog."

"Where's Dad and Beth?"

"With Wally and Aileen."

Wally and Aileen have been our neighbours since we moved here. They've lived in Hebden Bridge forever. Wally was in the army, and Aileen was a seamstress. They are our grandparents. Not by blood, but in every way that counts. Mum and Dad lost their parents young. I vaguely remember my grandma on my mum's side. That's about it. Aileen and Wally were, and are, the ones we look to for that relationship. They're both in their late seventies and share a birthday. Married for sixty years, and genuinely two of the best people I have ever known.

"I'll pop over in a bit. Just need to get everything upstairs and then somehow get Liam and Reggie inside."

"Oh boy. They're going to be soaked."

"Yup." I laugh.

"Well, Liam has been nonstop chattering about you arriving, so if he's happy, that's all that matters."

Ah bugger it, my clothes can wait. I need some family time, and nothing is better than a quick snowball fight with my brother and nutty dog.

Mum sees the gleam in my eye and grins. "Go on, I'll sort your bags."

Kissing her on the cheek, I shuffle back to the door, almost toppling over myself trying to get my winter boots on. I've only just stepped out when something cold and hard smacks me straight in the face. Liam's howl of laughter and Reggie's yaps of excitement pull me from my stunned, frozen spot on the porch step.

"Oh, you're going down, dude!" I yell, followed by an impressive war cry.

# December 2nd

M y plan to spend time with the family failed spectacularly. As soon as I'd been pulverised by Liam and his ridiculously sharp snowball aim, I took myself upstairs to shower and change, where I promptly fell asleep, missing dinner and my first evening with everyone. In my defence, I had just worked a full week, and my brain clearly needed to shut off for a while. Let's not forget Steph and that shit show, either.

So, now it's the second of December, and I have more time to make up for. My pre-millennium alarm clock tells me it's almost half-eight. Mum will be at the tea shop already, and Dad will be doing something woodwork-y in his shed. Dad retired last year, after thirty years in the police force. He now dedicates his days to drinking tea, painting birdhouses, and building ukeleles.

Despite my messy hair and smeared makeup, I confidently go in search of coffee in my reindeer onesie. My family has seen me in worse states over the years.

"Morning love," Mum calls.

"What are you doing here?"

"Nice to see you too." She chuckles. "Niamh is looking after the shop today. I wanted to spend some time with you."

"Ah, you didn't have to do—Niamh?"

"Oh, yes, I didn't tell you, did I?"

"Didn't tell me what?"

"She's back. Moved in with her mum a few months ago."

Well, that's a blast from the past. Niamh, pronounced Neev, is a childhood friend who moved back to Ireland ten years ago. We kept in touch, but the communication petered out after a couple of years. We weren't super close; she was Liam's buddy more than mine. She was about the only one who stuck around after his accident. When she knew he was going to be okay, Niamh took a job in Dublin. Something to do with brewing, I think.

"Why did she move back?" I pour myself a gigantic mug of coffee, drowning it in cream and sugar.

"Not sure, love. All I know is she needed a job, and I needed some help."

"Has she seen Liam?"

"Oh yes, they're thick as bloody thieves." Mum laughs, shaking her head. "Liam is so happy she's back."

There's not much more to add to the conversation, so I inhale my caffeine instead of making idle chitchat. That's the wonderful thing about my family. They don't push me to speak. I've always been more reserved than my siblings. Liam is the perpetually positive middle child. Beth is the wild youngest, and I'm the sensible eldest.

Suitably hopped up on Peruvian dark blend, I help Mum clean the kitchen. Having us all at home is no effortless task. The woman is a saint in my eyes. "Where's Beth?"

"War Room."

Scoffing, I throw down the holly embroidered tea towel. "I can't believe she didn't wait. Is Liam there too?"

"Yup."

Stalking off, I head towards the cellar door, aka the War Room. Mum and Dad had it converted into a lounge space for us kids. It had nothing to do with our comfort and everything to do with them needing space. We kids were over the moon. Having our very own HQ was friggin' epic growing up.

Securing the door behind me, I descend the wooden stairs. Liam and Beth are bent over the table we installed a few years ago, nattering between themselves.

"You could have waited," I moan. Oh, how quickly we slip into teenagers. I'm 37, yet a few seconds with these guys and I'm a prepubescent with acne all over again.

"It's not our fault you're old and need a bazillion hours of sleep," Beth shoots, her eyes alive with mischief. Liam giggles. I smile and stand for a second to take in my baby sister. She's tall like me. All three of us get that from our dad. Mum's on the short side. I inherited Mum's blonde hair, whereas Liam and Beth are closer to redheads like Dad.

Unlike my tame, straight hair that usually lives in a ponytail, Beth's hair is a short bob of wild curls. "You look good, Beth," I say, striding over and taking her in my arms.

We haven't seen each other in a year. Beth moved to Scotland with her boyfriend Ted three years ago. She's a vet, and he's a sheep farmer. I never thought my sister would settle in the countryside, but by the looks of her, she's thriving.

"Hey," Liam whines as we continue to hug.

Opening my arm, I pull the much larger sibling into us. His beefy arms wrap us up and squeeze a tad too hard. As soon as we've broken free and helped each other realign our spines, Beth hands me a lukewarm hot chocolate. It's tradition to start Operation Sleigh Bells with hot chocolate and gingerbread.

"Okay Robinsons, where are we up to?"

Beth circles the map on the table. It is a detailed representation of our street and the surrounding area. This map has taken us close to a decade to make. Each year, we add a little more or erase something that has changed.

"I've added the Thompsons' new conservatory, although I can't see how that would be a viable place to use."

"Let's not rule anything out."

"What about the roofs?" Liam asks. "I think we need to watch the roofs."

Beth and I nod.

"Good thinking, buddy. I'll make a note." Scribbling his suggestion on my snowflake shaped notepad, I continue to study the map.

The Robinsons' Operation Sleigh Bells tradition started a year after Liam's accident. We've always spent the month of December together, ever since I moved out at eighteen. We're a close family and didn't want to lose that when we were no longer in proximity. Now, how to explain the rest without sounding bonkers?

Okay, so Mum has always been the queen of Christmas. She made the holiday so special it had a profound effect on all of us. The effort she'd put in to make Christmas magical was, and still is, astounding. As we grew up, obviously, we understood Santa wasn't the one leaving the sooty footprints by the fireplace, and the fat man and his reindeer weren't the ones eating the mince pie and carrot. However, there has always been one thing none of us kids could figure out. The sleigh bells. Exactly five days before Christmas, each of us would hear sleigh bells jingling. You know, like the ones on Santa's sleigh. Anyway, they were close, but not close enough to pinpoint exactly where they were located.

To this day, Mum won't tell us how she does it. And yes, it still happens. Last year, when Beth and I were on our way back from Wally and Aileen's, we heard them. Beth did a spectacular jump over the hedge in a bid to catch Mum red-handed, but it wasn't to be. No one was there.

We raced home, thinking we'd catch either her or Dad taking off their coat or something that incriminated them, but once again, we were thwarted. Mum and Dad were laughing their bums off at the *Morcombe and Wise Christmas Special* rerun. Their coats hadn't moved, nor had their shoes.

Before Liam's accident, we didn't do much to find answers. Sure, we'd pester Mum to tell us how she did it, but that was all. When Liam was well enough to come home from the hospital, we all vowed to make Christmas extra special for him. It was Liam who latched on to the sleigh bells mystery, convinced Santa was behind it.

Beth and I played along, but secretly we wanted to uncover how the hell Mum made sleigh bells ring every damn year without getting caught. So, that's how Operation Sleigh Bells was born. Every year since, Beth, Liam, and I come up with a plan to figure it out. Liam still thinks he's going to catch Santa, which is perfect, because why the hell shouldn't he believe in Saint Nick? Me and Beth just want to solve the bloody mystery once and for all.

Mum calls the cellar the War Room because that's what it looks like. We have different maps pinned to the walls with red crosses marking where each of us has heard sleigh bells over the years.

Beth has done a fabulous job of cross-referencing Mum's whereabout on those occasions, which wasn't easy considering we were trying to collect evidence from memories. So far, we have nothing. Every time, Mum has an alibi. We turned our attention to Dad as well, because Mum obviously has an accomplice, but he too had solid alibis.

This year is the year, though. I can feel it. We will crack the sleigh bells case wide open. However, we have no intention of ruining this for Liam, so Beth and I will keep the truth to ourselves.

We have eighteen days to prepare.

We lose Liam to his Xbox two hours into planning. Beth is feverishly writing fresh ideas of how to snare Mum, which sounds bad, I know.

"What if we split up?" I say.

"We did that in 2016, remember? It didn't work then, so it's not gonna work now. Mum's too crafty."

"When is Ted getting here?"

"Twenty-first."

"We could ask him to help us. Like a spy or something."

Beth snorts. "Ted loves Mum way too much to nark on her. He's on the enemy's side."

"Well...what about Niamh?" Why didn't I think of it sooner?

"I can ask her," Liam shouts over the current bombing raid he's committing on whatever shoot-'em-up game he's playing. I haven't even answered before he's pressing the call button on his phone. Niamh must be on his speed dial.

"Nim, it's Liam."

Liam started calling Niamh Nim after his accident. He couldn't reconcile how Niamh's name was spelled to how it sounded, so with Niamh's blessing, he started calling her Nim. It saved us all a lot of anxiety, because Liam would get frustrated and angry when he couldn't read her name.

"Nim, come here, please. We need you in the War Room."

I look at Beth and smile. Liam is so serious as he talks, anyone would think we were strategising to halt an invasion or something.

"Yes, okay, after work. Can I have a scone?" Always thinking with his stomach. "Yes, fruit and jam. Thanks Nim, bye."

It's doubtful he gave her a chance to sign off before he pressed the end call button.

He grins. "She will be here in an hour."

"Good job, Liam. We might just do it this year." I wink at him.

"I'm not sure she'll be loyal to us," Beth comments, tapping the pen on her chin.

"Why wouldn't she be? She's Liam's best friend, and, if memory serves, was just as keen as us at one point to figure it out."

"Yeah, but Mum's her boss now. She could be a double agent."

"Lunch is served," Mum bellows from the door.

We take a second huddle. "Okay Robinsons, it's go-time. From now on we are to observe all of Mum and Dad's comings and goings. Note down anything strange. I'll start with a sweep of the house. Those bells have to be here somewhere."

"Liam, remember, Mum and Dad work for Santa, so you can't tell them if you find a clue."

"I won't Nic. I'll come to you and Beth. And Nim. And Reggie. Can Reggie be my partner?"

"Of course. I've been training him for you." Not a total lie. I attempted to get him to react to sleigh bells a few weeks ago, but that went terribly. It just resulted in him losing his shit every time a doorbell chimed. Steph wasn't impressed.

"Ready on three," I call. We pump our combined fists, shouting, "Robinsons rock," loudly. I hear Mum laughing. She's used to it by now.

"Are we really doing this again?" Mum asks, as we sit down together. Dad is already feeding Reggie bits of ham from his plate.

"Doing what?" Beth replies nonchalantly.

"You'll never figure it out." Mum grins, infuriating us immediately. She's so confident.

"This year is the year." I mock glare.

"No, it's not, and do you know why?" We shake our collective heads in sync. "Because the sleigh bells are magic."

Goddamn it!

Halfway through pudding, the doorbell rings, sending Reggie off the deep end. There's nothing I can do, so I just sit there waiting for Dad to answer the door. As soon as my rambunctious dog knows there is someone new in the house, that will distract him and he'll calm down.

Or not. Now he's barking and zooming through the house. I think I broke him.

"Afternoon all." The thick Irish accent pulls me up short before I even lay eyes on Niamh. She always had a slight accent, but it's a thousand times stronger now, and it's lovely. I'm one of those people that certain accents do very peculiar things to certain parts of their bodies. Irish is the accent that does it for me.

Lowering my fork, I turn in my chair. Niamh is standing there looking...well, bloody amazing. Holy baubles, ten years have done amazing things to that woman. Niamh was always a looker, with rich black hair and green eyes. But, for whatever reason, I find her completely captivating now. She's smaller than me by two or three inches but makes that up in heeled boots. Her jeans are snug to shapely legs. I can't see what top she's got on through her buttoned-up peacoat, but I'm sure it's just as lovely as her other clothes.

"Nic!" Beth's hand clipping me 'round the head brings me back to the room, and I want the floor to open up and swallow me. Everyone is staring at me, including Niamh. "I said, you remember Niamh, right?"

"Don't be stupid, of course I do. Hey." My little wave in her direction does nothing to stop the embarrassment of two bright red blushing cheeks. Awesome.

"Nim, come with me," Liam says, entirely unaware of anything that just happened. Niamh happily takes his hand and retreats down the hall to the War Room without another word.

"What the bloody hell was that?" Beth laughs, punching me in my arm.

"What was what?"

"I thought we were going to have to pop your eyeballs back in for a minute there, kid." Dad laughs. Oh, how very hilarious for them all.

"Leave her be," Mum chides, although I can see she's repressing a smirk.

"Yeah, leave me be. I was just surprised to see her, is all. Now, can I finish my lunch in peace?"

"No," Beth barks. "War Room. Now."

Liam is showing Niamh the map when Beth and I trudge down the stairs. I try to radiate confidence, but I know I'm failing. I'm a bit of a wet rag when it comes to pretty women. They make me flustered. It's amazing I've had so many girlfriends, really.

Beth heads straight on over to the chattering pair, giving me a much-needed parcel of space. My eyes wander to the far wall near the TV. As a joke, Beth started an advent calendar for me. It's not as nice as it sounds. She made it so that I opened a door every time I got dumped before Christmas. Guess I'll go open door number seventeen then.

"Hey," Niamh's soft voice says right next to my ear. I was so caught up in the calendar I didn't see her walk over to me. Now, I'm a steady kind of woman. My nerves aren't usually a problem. I'm a firefighter for god's sake, but they fail me now, as I make a shrieking noise worthy of Reggie, when Niamh speaks.

"Jesus," I pant.

"Yeah, I'd say so. Jumpy much." Niamh laughs.

"I didn't see you there, sorry."

"My fault. I just wanted to say hello properly. It's been a while, Nicole Robinson."

"It has indeed, Niamh O'Conner. I hear you're back from Ireland."

"Aye, it's true. Needed a change, so thought I'd come back here. You're looking really well. Still in the business of putting out fires?"

"Yep, and still loving it."

"And still trying to figure out the bells?"

If it were anyone else, I'd think they were making a dig, or taking the piss, but not with Niamh. She knows what this means to us, especially Liam. "This is the year."

"Liam wants to recruit me as a spy." She smiles.

"And what do you think? Are you up for the challenge? It would be a perilous task, going up against Mrs Robinson."

She takes a small step towards me. "They don't call me nimble Nim, for nothing you know." My brain freezes. Just how nimble is she? "You know, because I can sneak about without being caught," she adds, grinning, and I know she did it on purpose to trip me up.

I have a sneaking suspicion sleigh bells are going to be the least of my worries over the next few days.

# December 3rd

We spent the rest of yesterday bringing Niamh up to speed. She was more than thrilled to get involved in our quest to solve the sleigh bells. I tried to keep a respectable distance from her, because in all honesty I knew I'd get tongue-tied and make an arse of myself if I didn't.

Today, I plan to help Mum out at the tea shop for a few hours. My days here can't be all sleigh bells and silliness. I'm more than aware Mum works hard all day and then comes home to my dad and Liam. Having an adult child who needs permanent care is tough. That's why I do what I can while I'm here, things like working at the shop or doing minor DIY jobs. Dad covers the majority of stuff like that, but he's not exactly a spring chicken anymore.

Beth is lounging on the sofa, throwing individual chocolate Nesquik balls in her mouth. Liam is sitting on the floor, attention fully devoted to the game he's playing. Neither pays an ounce of attention to me as I grab my coat and shoes. It's not easy being the eldest at times. Always feeling the weight of responsibility sitting on your shoulders.

Mum's tea shop, The Soggy Biscuit—I begged her not to call it that—is only a five-minute drive away. Nestled in the heart of the town in an old Yorkshire block building. There is something about Yorkshire stone that makes me feel at home.

Finding a parking space is akin to winning the lottery, and yet I snag a space only a few hundred yards from the shop. Winner! The walk gives me time to take in the place. I can't believe it's been a year since I've walked these streets.

The council has done a fantastic job with the Christmas lights strung up between the buildings and around the old-fashioned streetlamps. The scene could easily moonlight as the set of a Victorian TV show. I listen to the ducks chattering away with each other on the canal.

People mill about in warm clothes, clutching takeout cups of my mum's famous hot chocolate. The air smells like Christmas and baked goods.

The Soggy Biscuit is crammed, with people lining up outside waiting to gain entrance. Mum has decorated the two large windows with a nice touch of fake snow and holly leaf decals. The patrons waiting in the bitter cold take turns pushing their faces up against the glass to see if the queue is moving along. I'm not surprised I get several raised eyebrows and under-breath complaints as I push past them all to squeeze myself inside.

Michael Bublé plays softly in the background, although I doubt many people can hear him over the din. It's a Tuesday, and yet no one looks like they're scurrying off to work anytime soon.

"Oh Nic, love, thank goodness. Could you grab an apron and help clear some tables?"

"On it, Mum!" The dagger-staring customers suddenly withdraw their contempt at letting me pass by and instead part the way like I'm a queen. Anything to get their chocolate faster, I see.

Throwing my coat haphazardly through the staff room door, I grab a Soggy Biscuit apron and get to work.

Having worked here on and off for years, I take but a second to get in the groove.

As soon as I've cleared a table off, someone is anxiously hovering next to me, hoping I'll bugger off so they can claim the prized spot. Suppressing a grin, I shuffle out of the way, not wanting to be the focus of an impatient customer.

Maybe an hour goes by before the place finally becomes manageable. I'm used to heavy lifting and strenuous work, but even I'm feeling a tad tired. Mum leans up against the counter after serving the last frozen punter. His hot chocolate will thaw him out.

"Phew, thanks, honey. You came in just at the right time. Here, have a drink." Mum offers me a humongous mug filled to the brim with creamy hot chocolate. She then hands me the spray cream, because she's the best mum in the world.

"Come and sit with me for five minutes," I say. Nodding, Mum makes herself a cup of strong Yorkshire tea and joins me at the table closest to the back of the room. "I didn't know this place was doing so well!"

Mum shrugs, then grins. "It's all because of Niamh. She was only here a day before she started telling me about the potential of attracting new customers if we were a little more present online."

"Social media?"

"Yup. Well, you know me and technology. Haven't got the first bloody clue, so I asked if she could take over that part, and she said yes. And well, you can see the results. Less than a week later, people started pouring in, and it hasn't stopped."

"Well, you serve the best tea and hot chocolate in Yorkshire."

"It would seem so!" Mum takes a few sips of her tea, all the time eyeing me. "I'm glad Stephanie didn't come. She wasn't good enough for you." The hot chocolate I've just swallowed gets inhaled into my lungs. Mum leans over and gives me a few good wallops on the back.

"What?" I splutter, still trying not to choke to death.

"Well, it's true. You know I don't enjoy interfering in your private life, sweetie. You're a grown woman, but this one... She was no good."

"Um..."

"Now, someone like Niamh..."

Good lord, is she trying to do me in? My whole family is supportive of me, and always have been ever since I accidentally came out to them at sixteen. I had my first girlfriend over for tea, no one the wiser she was, in fact, my girlfriend. That was until I completely lost my mind and squeezed her bum as I walked her to the door.

I hadn't even realised what I'd done until I waved her off, closed the front door and turned to face my entire family. Mum's eyebrows were up somewhere in her hair. Beth shouted, 'busted' repeatedly. Liam laughed and told me that Kelly—the aforementioned girlfriend—*did* have a nice bum, and then Dad turned bright red because, and I quote, "No father wants to see their child getting amorous." Amorous! I mean, really.

After what felt like ten years of pure embarrassment, Mum and Dad finally sat me down, telling me in no uncertain terms there was zero problem, and they loved me. That was that. Throughout my teens and well into my twenties, Mum and Dad welcomed women I brought home, never sharing their opinions, allowing me to make up my mind and live my life. So, you can understand why Mum's sudden need to weigh in is a shock.

"Mum, Niamh...no, I mean, she's, you know...but no."

"Wow, that was smooth, kiddo. Don't think I didn't see your face when she walked in yesterday."

"Okay, fine, she's...pretty—"

"She's gorgeous, give over!"

"Mum, she's also Liam's best friend."

"And?"

"I'm only here for a few weeks. What's the point? And she might not even be interested!"

"Who is not interested in who?" Niamh's Irish lilt makes me shiver involuntarily.

"Hmm?" Mum replies. "Oh, nothing, dear. Just girl talk. I thought I gave you the day off?"

"You did, but I was jonesing for a decent cup of tea."

"Join us. I'll grab a pot." Mum is up and away before anyone has a chance to open their mouths. It's her specialty.

"She's got you working too?"

I smile and try to mask my rising temperature at the sight of her. Again, she's dressed in tight black jeans, boots and, as I can now see, a lovely knit sweater. Hanging her coat on the back of the seat, Niamh sits in the chair next to me. Far too close for comfort, I might add.

Mum has only sat down a second with a fresh pot of tea when an unfamiliar voice startles me from my obvious ogling.

"Niamh, there you are." Mum and I turn to look at the person talking. She's tall, with cropped blonde hair, sporting a flannel and ripped jeans. It doesn't take a seasoned lesbian to see she's in the club.

I watch as she leans down and kisses Niamh straight on the mush. Mum's eyes snap to me in obvious surprise. I look everywhere but at Niamh and whoever the hell this person is.

"Pat, what are you doing here? I thought we were meeting in half an hour by the canal?"

"I couldn't wait to see you."

Ew, barf. My face must betray my feelings because Mum swiftly boots me in the shin.

"Shit! Ow!"

Niamh turns to me with questioning eyebrows. "Knocked the table," I mumble.

"Sorry, how rude. Mrs Robinson, Nic, this is Pat."

Pat salutes. "Nice to meet you. I've heard a lot about your family." I don't like *that* one bit. "I'll grab a drink and be back in a second."

Mum signals Beccy to serve Pat. "And who is Pat?" she not so subtly asks Niamh.

"I met her two weeks ago at a bar. We're sort of dating."

"Sort of, but not exclusively." It's my turn to do the shin kicking.

Niamh laughs. "Well, we haven't talked about it. It's a little too early."

"What did I miss, lovely people?" Pat plonks herself down, astride the chair she scraped over from another table.

"Nothing. I'd only just got here myself," Niamh replies.

My throat seems to have taken my voice hostage. Weird and unfamiliar feelings are manifesting in my chest and stomach.

Without missing a beat, Pat forges on, "So, you're the family that does an entire month of stuff together, right?"

"We spend December together, yes." Mum smiles, but I see it's tight, and not her natural one.

Pat turns to me. "And you actually use up all your allotted holiday days to do that?"

"Yes," I answer, feeling my jaw tighten.

"Right. Cool, to each their own. And there's something about bells?" I see Niamh blanch, then her face flush.

"Right, lovely to meet you Pat, but I need to get back." Standing, I give Mum a quick kiss on the cheek, and hastily make my exit without looking at Niamh or Pat again.

The drive home is less than blissful. I'm pissed. I thought Niamh was different, but clearly not. She gets her kicks by laughing about our family tradition, just like everyone else who doesn't understand. What is the big fucking deal? We celebrate and have family time for a month. So what?

Reggie greets me first with manic barking and two muddy paws. He's been in the garden digging and no one thought to wash him off. Sweeping him up, I stomp off to the bathroom. The time alone gives me a chance to cool off. I don't really know why I'm so upset. Everyone I've met thinks our family tradition is too much. Why should Niamh be any different? And why couldn't Dad or Beth have washed my dog? Okay, that's my anger being redirected. I'm cognisant enough to understand my own feelings.

With Reggie displaying *his* feelings of being bathed to the entire street, I give him one last wash and start drying him.

"Jesus, why's he making that racket?" Beth asks from the bathroom door.

"He doesn't like water," I huff.

"What's got in your knickers?"

"Couldn't you have washed him? You obviously let him outside to dig."

"Dad did."

"Does it matter? I've been at the tea shop with Mum all day and know I have to come back and start clearing up after everyone. Fuck's sake, Beth. Would it kill you or Dad to bloody help out once in a while?"

"Whoa," Mum says from behind Beth. I didn't even hear her come home. "Beth, tell your dad to get dinner on, please."

Beth side-eyes me, confused and hurt at my outburst. She looks at Mum who shakes her head. When Beth is downstairs, Mum walks in, takes the towel from my hand and lets Reggie bolt out the door. "Let's have a chat."

Ugh, why can your mum still make you feel like a child with just a few words and the tone of her voice? We head to my room, where I scramble onto my bed. "Sorry."

"What was that about?"

"I was just irritated. You've got to admit, Mum, that Beth and Dad could help a bit more."

"Your dad helps plenty, and you know Beth spends most of her time with Liam."

"So do I, and I help at the tea shop!"

"Yes, which you don't have to do, love."

"You need help!"

"I have help. Nic, I wish you didn't feel you have to take everything on in this family."

"I don't, but while we're here, we should help you out. I don't think that's asking too much considering everything you do for us, Mum."

She shuffles up the bed and places a hand on my cheek. "You are so wonderfully thoughtful, honey. But I want you to enjoy yourself while you're here. And honestly, it makes me feel good to dote on you all again. That's why I love December so much. I get all my babies back."

Sighing, I rub my forehead. "Sorry. I'll apologise to Beth."

"Don't worry too much. I'll have a word with her. Now, do you want to talk about what happened in the shop?"

"Nothing happened. Niamh thinks our traditions are silly, just like everyone else who knows about them."

"I didn't hear her say that."

"Why else would she feel the need to tell a perfect stranger about it and the bells? We're just a fun titbit to pass around when a conversation needs starting. I was just surprised to find out Niamh is the type of person to do that, I guess."

"I don't think it's like that, sweetie."

"It doesn't matter. I'm not here for her. Shall we go down and see what the other Robinsons are up to?"

Sensing my need to move on from this conversation, Mum pulls me up and drags me downstairs where I quickly mumble an apology to Beth, who hugs me and says she'll help out more. Liam is on the floor with Reggie wrestling.

After a scrumptious plate of steak and ale pie, Beth, Liam, and I set ourselves up in the War Room. We always make Christmas cards for each other and our parents. But as we got older, our designs got more outrageous and naughty. I couldn't display some cards Beth gave me over the years, unless I had an 18+ sign pinned up somewhere. It gives us all a laugh, though.

Once we've finished adult arts and crafts, we all settle in to watch some crap telly. I've all but put the day's earlier mishap behind me when the doorbell rings. Reggie goes insane, Liam laughs hysterically at the dog zooming around the living room and I clamp my hands over my ears. I'm going to have to hire a dog trainer in the new year.

Mum comes back from the hallway after answering the door with a grin on her face. Trailing behind her is Niamh, looking directly at me. I look at the floor. "Visitor," Mum states unnecessarily.

"Nim, you here to play?" Liam asks enthusiastically.

"Not tonight, Liam. I just need a quick word with your sister, if that's okay?"

"Beth, Nim wants to talk to you."

"I meant the other sister." Niamh chuckles.

"Nic, Nim wants to talk to you."

"Thanks, buddy. I heard."

Well, this should be interesting.

# December 4th

It's 12:07 a.m., officially making it the fourth of December, and Niamh is still here. In my room. After agreeing to talk, we went upstairs, and she immediately settled on my bed and asked if we could watch a movie. I was so stunned I just nodded, walked over to my flatscreen and pulled up *Chicken Run*—because that's my go-to Christmas film—even though Beth tells me it isn't actually a festive movie. Whatever.

So, we watched *Chicken Run* and then the second. Niamh asked if we could have popcorn. I dumbly nodded again and went to make some. Mum, Dad, and Beth looked at me expectantly and I just shrugged, way too off-centre to answer questions they may have had.

We ate the popcorn in amiable silence, watching *Wallace & Gromit,* although my head was far from quiet. Finally, at 12:06 a.m. Niamh turns to me. "Can I stay over?"

As I said, it's now…12:07 a.m. and I'm yet to answer. My behaviour comes across as discomfort because Niamh is trying to backtrack now. "Sorry, that was weird. I'll just go."

Sticking my hand out, I grab some part of her arm. "No, it's fine, and of course you can stay. Um, I can take the floor."

"The bed's big enough for us both, Nic."

Is she having me on?

"Sure." I go to open my mouth to ask her…something, anything that would explain this situation, but she's already on her feet heading to the bathroom. I take her absence as an opportunity to speed through my nightly routine, which doesn't take much, to be honest. I'm not the three lotions to the face kind of woman. I'll moisturise my legs now and then, but that's about it.

My elf slippers and matching pyjama set scream immaturity, but the alternative is worse. I usually sleep nude or in a tank top that is threadbare. Neither is an option, so elves it is.

Niamh sweeps back in fresh-faced, and then it hits me. I was so worried about what *I* would wear to bed I didn't even think about what *she* would wear! Rushing past with a small smile, I head to the bathroom, scrub my teeth, and douse my face in cold water.

Back in my bedroom, where Niamh freaking O'Conner is waiting for me, I take a second to tidy up. When I say tidy up, I mean awkwardly move one thing from the floor to the chair in the corner of the room. I can feel her eyes on me and the smirk plastered on her face.

"Are you coming to bed?" I hope the squeak of longing I made in my head remained inside. Otherwise that's embarrassing. But, hey, I'm a hot-blooded lesbian with a penchant for women with an Irish accent. I think I'm doing a marvellous job of keeping it together, all things considered.

Nodding my head like an idiot, I slide under the covers where Niamh is already situated. She's wearing a t-shirt, which I presume was under her jumper. What about the bottom half? Lying prone like a corpse, I pull the duvet up to my chin. It's a fabulous Wednesday Addams impression. Niamh is silent, and I daren't look. So, I gaze at the pizza stain on my roof. Beth and I had a food fight a few years ago after one too many eggnogs. It took me days to find and clean all the morsels of pizza. Looks like I missed a spot.

The gentle sigh that escapes Niamh's lips has me melting and freezing to the spot at the same time.

"Nic," she says, oh-so-quietly, it's almost a whisper in the air. I turn my face robotically because I believe my brain is broken. Niamh is lying on her side, her hands under the pillow, her eyes looking over my face, searching. But for what? "I'm sorry about earlier."

"Nothing to be sorry for." Yes, I was upset earlier, but now I couldn't summon the ire to melt a snowflake, let alone be mad at her.

"You were upset. I could see it." Turning my face back to the ceiling, I give a small shrug of the shoulders. I don't know what to say. "Nic, I wasn't gossiping or making fun of your family when I told Pat. You know, or I hope you do, that I love this tradition you guys have. Actually, its been something I've looked forward to since getting back."

"Okay."

"Can you use more words?" Her tone is soft, but I can hear the amusement laced in it.

Huffing, I turn back to her, this time allowing my whole body to move. "Yeah, I was upset. It pisses me off when people make fun of our tradition, especially when it's got nothing to do with them."

"In her defence, I don't think Pat meant to ridicule you or your family. I think she was genuinely curious."

"That may be so, but I still feel under a spotlight when all the questions inevitably start. No offence to your girlfriend, Nim, but I don't want to explain everything to her, just so she gets it."

"I'd never want or expect you to. And she's not my girlfriend."

"The person you're dating, then."

"Is there more to this? I've never known you to get so worked up over other people's opinions."

I chuckle. "Niamh, you haven't seen me in ten years. People change."

"Not that much. You're still the person I knew all those years ago."

"How do you know?"

"I knew it as soon as I saw you again."

The air is heady with something I can't put a name to. But it's something very unexpected. Niamh is watching me so intensely my heart picks up its pace.

I come to my senses in time to avert a guaranteed mistake. Niamh is just apologising, and I would ruin it by misinterpreting her signals. I've done that before, and I'm always the one with egg on my face in the end.

"Steph, my girlfriend, broke up with me the day we were supposed to come here." Talking about an ex is a surefire way to break the tension.

"I'm sorry," she says, her hand reaches from under the pillow to land delicately on my abdomen. Thank god for the duvet creating a much-needed barrier.

"She tried to give me an ultimatum. Her or the Christmas tradition with my family."

Niamh takes a sharp breath in, her eyes turning from soft to hard in an instance. "That's bullshit!"

The expletive takes me by surprise, as does the thickness of her accent. I can't help but laugh.

"Yeah, and that's why she's no longer my girlfriend. I suppose I was still reeling from that when Pat opened her mouth." Oops, that sounded bitchy. "I mean... Sorry, that sounded harsh."

"No, Pat has a tendency to do that I'm learning."

"So, you like her then? Obviously, if you're dating her."

"She's fun, but I can't see things going long-term. I'm ready to build a life. The last few years have been a little rough."

"Are you okay?" This, talking to Niamh in the dead of the night, is...really nice.

"Yeah, I left Ireland after a bad break-up. Despite being separated for about a year, our social circles were closely intertwined. I couldn't escape her, and...well, she wasn't the nicest person."

"Did she hurt you?" I feel *my* anger rising now.

"Not physically. Anyway, I made the call to come home. I wasn't looking for anyone to be with. It's been nice standing on my own two feet for a change. But Mum was getting at me about being alone all the time, so I caved and went to a bar. That's where I met Pat. She's outgoing and fun, but not in a place where she wants a house, pets, and maybe kids one day. I mean, I'm getting up in age now—"

"Hey." I laugh. "You're only thirty-four. If that's getting up in age, what the hell am I?"

"Oh yeah, I forget you're the old one." Her eyes crinkle as she snickers to herself. I mock huff and pretend I'm turning my back on her, which causes her hand to grip the duvet hard, blocking any movement. "Don't get your knickers in a twist. You still look good for an old fogey."

We both laugh out loud until I remember everyone is asleep and will murder us if we wake them. I shush us until there is only a low giggle permeating the silence.

"Anyway, as I was saying. I want to look for *the one*, you know."

"Yeah." I sigh. "I sometimes think it's impossible."

"Why?" I feel her shift ever so slightly closer.

"I'm not sure, to be honest. I just know that I've had a lot of girlfriends, and none of them ever came close to being *the one*. Did you see the Christmas calendar on the wall in the War Room?"

"Yeah, I couldn't work it out."

"It's a special one, courtesy of Beth. I open a door every time I get dumped. She thinks it's hilarious. I'm on door seventeen this time 'round. Although that's okay, two years ago I had to open three doors. It was depressing as hell."

"Shite, I'm sorry."

"What for?"

"For you having to do that every year. It's a little insensitive on Beth's part, don't ya think?"

Yeah, I do, but I know it's only meant to be a bit of fun. "It's fine. Hopefully, I won't get to door twenty-four."

"I think you'll find her. Ms Right."

"She has to be okay with me being here every December."

"Is that usually a problem?"

Barking out a much too loud laugh, I shake my head. "Oh yes, that's a problem. I think every one of my relationships has ended because I do this every year."

"Are you shitting me?" So, Niamh curses when she's angry. Good to know.

"Nope, no shitting. It's a genuine issue. I mean, I get it. I know our arrangement isn't usual. Seeing someone's parents for weeks on end is far from ideal for most. I've always maintained that my partners didn't have to come, but that causes problems in and of itself. I'm getting to the point of giving up. Maybe I'd be better off alone, with Reggie."

"Don't say that. You're going to make some lucky woman...well, really lucky."

"Maybe." Snuggling down in the bed, I feel my eyes growing heavy. Emotional conversations always exhaust me.

"Are we okay?" Niamh asks.

"Of course we are."

"I'm...sorry about the impromptu sleepover. I came here to apologise and then leave, but I couldn't think of what to say. That's why I asked to watch a film. I thought I'd come up with the words, and then...it got late, and I enjoy hanging out with you. Is that sad?"

Smiling, I shake my head. "It's not sad. It's been a nice, if not a surprising, evening. I never thought I'd have a sleepover close to forty."

"Do you not have ladies stay over?" Niamh arcs an eyebrow, smirking.

"Not one where clothes stay on." I laugh. "Now, go to sleep. I'm grouchy if I don't get enough hours." I say that simply because I cannot handle any flirting or even the hint of flirting from this woman.

Rolling over to face away from Niamh, I close my eyes tightly and do my best to meditate. It must work at some point because when I wake up, it's daylight and I'm full-on spooning Niamh. She's on her front, facing away. One leg bent, both arms tucked under the pillow. I'm half on top of her, for crying out loud. My leg hooked over her thigh, my arm circling her waist, head buried in her neck. I mean for the love of beans. What was my unconscious self thinking? You know what I mean!

Prying myself off her as gently as possible, I slither out of my bed like I'm made of jelly. Slinking to the floor, I crawl silently to the door, swiping my onesie as I go. If Niamh wakes up now, I'm not sure how to explain what I'm doing. It's fine though. I make it to the upstairs hallway without disturbing her. Crawling face-first into my sister's shins is an unforeseen consequence.

"Do I want to know?" she croaks. Her voice is sleep addled.

"Nope." Jumping to my feet, I silently close my bedroom door and turn to go downstairs.

"You're seriously not going to tell me what that was about?"

"What, what was about?" Mum asks as we enter her domain. Food is already piled on the table.

"Nothing," I reply, knowing full well I'm not getting out of it.

"I just caught Nic crawling out of her room. Literally, crawling."

Mum stops stirring whatever is in the pot on the stove and turns to me, her lips sucked into her mouth. Is she trying to stop herself from laughing? Yes, clearly.

"I said it's nothing. I just—"

"Nim stayed in Nic's room," Liam announces. His six-foot frame is no quiet mouse coming down the stairs. More like a herd of reindeer. "In her bed," he adds.

Beth swivels her head like the exorcist girl, a shit-eating grin on her face. "Did she now."

I roll my eyes, feigning nonchalance. "We watched some movies, and it got late, so she stayed over. That's it. Everyone can return to their lives now."

"Morning," Niamh chimes, looking utterly devastating in my spare onesie. It's decorated with Christmas unicorns. "Something smells good."

If she's noticed my family reacting like they've just witnessed Santa himself popping by, she doesn't say or do anything to let on.

"No need to stand on ceremony. Dig in," Mum finally calls. Her eyes snap to me, and of course I blush. "What's on the agenda for today, my little cherubs?"

Beth rolls her eyes and smiles. I shake my head and laugh. Mum's terms of endearment are embarrassing and wonderful.

"What's a cherub?" Liam asks with toast hanging out of his mouth.

"An angel," Niamh replies.

"Okay. Nim, will you build a snowman with me?"

"Sure, that sounds like fun. Nic?" Her question catches me off guard. I do my best to chew and swallow the massive bite of bacon sandwich rolling around in my stuffed mouth.

"Sure," I half choke.

"Aces, I love a snowman day," Beth enthusiastically adds on.

I love a snowman day too, but now I don't think I'm going to relax at all. Nothing happened between us last night, but I think we got a little closer to friends. That would be nice if I could get other parts of my body to agree to a platonic relationship and not want so much more.

# December 5th

"Cooey," I call, letting myself into Wally and Aileen's house. They set the heat to a bazillion degrees, and every light in the house is on. We've always called out "Cooey." I don't know why. It's something Aileen has always said, and us kids picked up on it.

I feel super guilty. This is the first time I'm visiting them since getting back. I was going to pop over the first night but fell asleep. After that, I've had my head up my arse thinking about a certain Irish woman.

"There she is," Aileen calls, struggling to get out of her chair. I race over and bend down to receive my bone-crushing hug. Giving her a kiss on the cheek, I bounce over to Wally and receive the same treatment. He flashes a gummy smile, his dentures sitting on the small side table he keeps next to his recliner.

"I'm sorry it's taken me a few days to come over."

"Oh nonsense." Aileen waves my apology off. "You're here now. Want a cocoa?"

"You know I do."

Wally slips his teeth in, chomping down a few times to test them out. "Ail, I'll have one with a dash—"

"Of whiskey. Yes, dear."

Seeing them, smelling their house, being surrounded by their ancient furniture lightens my mood instantly. No matter what I'm going through, visiting Ail and Wal always brightens my day.

I make myself comfortable on the three-seater sofa neither of them ever use. Wal has one recliner and Aileen another. Wally is close to the TV and Aileen is close to the fire. It's always been the same. This house has been their home for over fifty years. They've updated nothing, despite our family's offer to help them out. They like it exactly the way it is.

Aileen and Wally couldn't have kids of their own, and they have no other family. So, when Mum and Dad moved in with me as a toddler, they doted on us and made us their own. All my memories as a child involve Aileen and Wal. Wally would take me and Beth to the cow fields to pick wild berries and collect shit for his flower beds. Aileen taught us how to cook vegetables fresh from their garden.

Mum and Dad worked full-time, so we spent most of our time after school with Aileen and Wally. We couldn't ask for better adopted grandparents.

Plus, they are a hoot at Christmas. Wally gets hammered off whiskey and yet still shows us all up for fools when we play Trivial Pursuit. Aileen gets tipsy and giggles at everything before becoming highly inappropriate. Some things she's told us about Wally in his prime...ugh, I shudder. Only strong alcohol numbs those memories.

"Here you go, love. Cocoa with a kick." Not only is there cocoa, but a tray of Fox's biscuits that only come out on special occasions. We sit in silence, watching *Coronation Street*, sipping our hot toddies.

We've done this a thousand times, and every time is special. I'm not blind to the fact they are getting old, so I want to bask in this—in them—for as long as possible. "No, Stephanie?" Aileen asks as soon as the show finishes.

"Nope."

"Good riddance," Wally pipes up. "She had weird eyebrows."

"Wal, behave or shut your trap." I can't help but giggle. "Never mind, sweetheart." Aileen pats my knee.

"I'm fine. Glad to be home."

"So, when do you want to search the house for the bells?"

My face heats immediately. I didn't come over here with the sole purpose of snooping, but Beth collared me before leaving the house, ordering me to start the search. "I... What?"

Wally belly laughs. "Oh Nic, you couldn't lie your way out of a paper bag, kiddo."

"I can save you the trouble and tell you there are no sleigh bells here, my sweet."

"Hmm, but that's what someone who wanted to keep the bells hidden would say!"

"She's got you there, Ail."

"Well, you're more than welcome to look."

Shaking my head, I drink more cocoa that has way more than a *dash* of whiskey. "Nope, you're expecting it now. I'm going to have to report back to Beth and Liam."

"Suit yourself." Aileen laughs. Aileen and Wal have been involved in our Christmas tradition from day one. We figured out it was Wal who called us on Christmas Eve pretending to be Santa. Still, no dice when it comes to those blasted bells.

"Have you been at the tea shop with your mum today?"

"I went in for a few hours this morning." As usual, it was crammed. Mum needs to get more people in if she wants to keep up this pace. "I did some shopping this afternoon." I spared Ail the details, but my mind drifted back to the earlier part of the day.

My goal for the day had been to get any last-minute Christmas shopping done before the town got completely chock-a-block. Plus, I hoped to find something for Niamh.

Everything started off well. I finished at the tea shop and meandered about for an hour or two, not really looking at anything. It was just nice to be out and about amongst lovely people. The one thing I'll say about the people in Yorkshire, they're a friendly bunch. People down south wouldn't know what to do with themselves if a random person suddenly said, "Good day" to them.

I ate too much junk. Greggs are my downfall and Mum might write me out of the will if she knew how many

Greggs sausage rolls I consume when I'm here. At home I'm very health conscious. But the second December starts, it's like my body craves carbs and fats. Mum doesn't help with all her baking, but the rest is my gluttonous arse indulging way too much.

So, three sausage rolls and a fatty mocha later, I began my serious search for presents. All the major gifts are still in the boot of my car. I like to pick up handcrafted bits and bobs from town to fill the family's stockings. I wondered if Niamh has a Christmas stocking?

With bags in hand, I was extremely happy with how the day was going until I rounded the corner and walked into Niamh and Pat, eating each other's faces. The sight was undoubtedly the worst thing I experienced in all my adult life. That might sound overly dramatic, but I kid you not.

My heart sank to my toes.

I know deep down the feelings I have for Niamh are one-sided. She's just friendly and I've taken it and morphed it into something unreal and unattainable, as proved by the fact she was snogging another woman.

My reaction was so strong that all I could focus on was getting the hell out of there. I could feel both pairs of eyes on me as I whirled 'round and ran smack into someone else. My bags scattered on the floor. It took several seconds to collect my things, all the time doing my level best to avoid eye contact. I glanced once at Niamh and she was bright red. That was clearly the theme of the month for me. I'd already lost count how many times I'd blushed these past five days.

Without a single word, I rushed away, choosing to head straight back to my parents' house and lock myself away for the rest of the day. Which is exactly what I did until I left to visit Aileen and Wally.

"Did you pick up anything nice?" I'm pulled from my less than pleasant memories by Aileen's wobbly voice.

"A few more gifts."

"How many sausage rolls did you eat?"

"Three." I mock sigh, as if it's the most shameful thing in the world.

"Ah, you've done worse. I think your record is six."

"Yeah, that was after a night of drinking, though."

"How's Niamh," Aileen blurts out of nowhere. Bloody hell, she's been henpecking with my mother. Or Beth, or both.

"I don't know. Why don't you tell me?" My snark is taken with a grin.

"According to my sources—"

"Mum."

"Sources I will not divulge. You had a little sleepover with the lovely Nim."

"It was nothing, as I've already informed my entire family. Anyway, she's seeing someone."

"Ah yes, the nosy Pat."

"Good Lord, you two are quicker than Twitter."

Crossing her arms over her chest, Aileen taps her foot. "Stop trying to change the subject."

"There isn't a subject to change. Niamh is seeing Pat, and from the kiss I saw them having today, I'd say they're getting serious." Even though Niamh said the opposite last night, I can't help but think she was either telling me fibs or unaware of how close she and Pat are, because no one kisses like that when it's only a fling. Well, not in my opinion.

"Poppycock," Wally barks. "They might have been sharing a kiss, but it was your bed she was in."

"We slept. That's it."

"Are you giving up already?" Aileen leans forward, her face giving me that stern I'm-about-to-tell-you-off-for-being-dumb look.

"Ail, there's nothing to give up on!"

"Young 'uns, I swear," she mumbles. "A woman doesn't randomly invite herself to stay over in your bed for no damn reason, Nic."

"It was la—"

"Uber. The local taxi rank. Hell, even your dad would have taken her home. She wanted to be there with you."

"Can we drop it, please?" It's not often I get irritated with Aileen, but she has a habit of grabbing onto something and not letting it go. What was my mother thinking? Toddling over here and sharing all that. Now I'm going to have to put up with invasive questions and unsolicited advice from Aileen until I go home. Great!

"Alright, I'll keep my gob shut," she huffs. "But I think you're being daft."

"Duly noted, thank you. Can we watch *Eastenders* in peace now?"

It's close to nine when I leave. Still rankled by Mum and Aileen's interference, I moodily trudge the twenty metres home. Beth is waiting on the doorstep in her coat. "About time. Jesus, *Eastenders* finished ages ago."

"I didn't know I had a curfew," I snap.

"Alright, that's twice in as many days you've snapped at me. We don't usually get to that part of the holiday season until at least the double digits in December. Last year we got all the way to the nineteenth before having a spat."

My shoulders slump. I can't keep taking my shitty mood out on my family. That's not right. Damn it. "Ugh, I'm sorry little sis. I suck."

"Yeah, ya do, but I'll forgive you if you buy me a pint. The Black Sheep is having a karaoke night, which will be hilarious."

"Done. But I'm not singing!"

"We'll see."

I end up singing. Beth is a master at getting me to do shit I don't want to do. However, there was little manipulative mastery in this case. Just three pints of Guinness.

We belt out *Islands in the Stream* by Kenny Rogers and Dolly Parton. I know that song backwards. I take Dolly's role only because she is my musical hero. Now, I'm not saying we're tone-deaf, but I definitely notice a few winces as we hit our stride. My throat is going to be raw in the morning.

After a hearty applause from a very sozzled crowd, Beth and I head back to our table, which has two fresh pints on it. Ah, god bless Yorkshire hospitality. When I'm about a third of the way through my drink, Beth suddenly sits up straight as if someone has wedged a stick up her backside.

"You okay?" I say, slurring ever so slightly.

"Yes. Shall we go home?"

"You never leave a drink half finished. What's up?" Her eyes wander over my shoulder and I get a creeping sensation up my neck. I know what, or who, I'm going to see when I turn around. Yep! There she is, Niamh, hand in hand with Pat. Perfect.

"For fuck's sake," I mumble.

"We can go," Beth whispers.

"No, we're here having a lovely night. Niamh can see whoever she wants. I'm not sure why everyone is acting so—"

"Hey, you two." Niamh is standing by our table, smiling down at us. My tipsy heart jolts at the mere sight of her.

"Hi." Good use of the English language.

"Nim, great to see you!" Beth all but screams. I bore a hole in her skull with my eyes, telling her to pipe the hell down.

Niamh simply laughs. "The Robinson sisters are a little tipsy, I see."

"Only a little." I smile.

"Oh hey, the Christmas family!" Ugh Pat.

Beth's face loses all joviality and zeroes in on Pat. Beth is not a good drunk. She's either way over the top happy or super pissy. By the scowl on her face, it's a pissy kinda night. "What's that supposed to mean?"

Pat smiles. "Nothing. Just you guys love Christmas, right? I mean, you'd have to if you wanted to put up with each other for so long. God, I'd kill my parents and brother if I spent more than a day with them."

"That's sad for you then," Beth growls.

"Beth, relax," I grind out through my teeth.

"Easy tiger," Pat replies, and my hackles raise.

"Pat," Niamh playfully scolds. "Leave them be."

"Babe, I'm only making conversation."

Babe? My arse, they're *just* dating. "You guys have an enjoyable night," I say, hoping they get the hint. Not that I don't want to spend time with Niamh, but neither Beth nor I are in the best state to take jabs about our Chrimbo plans.

I see Niamh's smile falter and I hate I did that to her, but it's for the best. "Oh, sure, thanks. Um, is it okay if I stop by tomorrow? Liam wanted me to go to the park with him."

"Of course. You don't have to ask." I smile, trying to make things right.

"Cool. I'm up for that, babe," Pat interrupts.

After Niamh doesn't correct Pat, letting her know she can't just invite herself to someone else's house, I decide this is where my evening ends. More alcohol will only lead to disaster.

Beth gathers her coat without me having to say anything. "Actually, you can have our table. We were just off."

I'm sure Niamh can see through such a flimsy excuse, but she doesn't say anything. "Night. I'll see you tomorrow."

"You two are leaving? Ah, that sucks. Okay, well, I'll see you tomorrow too, then."

We leave the pub, and I have to take a *very* deep breath to calm myself. These feelings are foreign, and I don't like them. I'm a little embarrassed by how I made up the connection I thought we shared last night in my head. It's not real, yet my feelings are acting as if they are.

"Come on, let's go raid Mum's sherry stash."

I love my sister.

# December 6th

"Up, up, up!"

Whaaaat is that horrendous noise? Is the world ending? My head feels like it's folding in on itself. "Mmm, nooo."

"Nic, Beth, move your arses!" That sounds like an irate...

"Stop being so loud." I hear Beth hiss. Everyone needs to shut up.

"I'm just going to get louder, the longer you keep me waiting, ladies." When Mum calls us *ladies* in that tone, we know we've fucked up. I just wish I could remember anything past leaving The Black Sheep pub. We couldn't have done anything good if we've made Mum bring out her "I'm-so-disappointed-in-you" voice.

I am suddenly expelled from wherever the hell I am. Hitting the floor with a good thump, I finally open my eyes and glare at whoever or whatever is in my line of sight. Beth is sitting up on the sofa, rubbing her eyes. I'm now on the floor by her feet, so I'll take a wild guess and say I fell asleep on her. We must look rough as a badger's arse. I certainly feel that way.

Scrambling to my feet at the pace of a snail and the balance of a baby giraffe, I try in vain to look like I have my life in order. Mum stands with hands on her hips, eyebrows raised. "Everything okay, Mum?"

Her scoff says everything. "Care to explain why my Christmas sherry is lacking its contents? Or why I have two traffic cones in my front garden, dressed in mine and your dad's clothing?"

Oh shit!

Beth is as helpful as a chocolate teapot as she bursts into laughter, rolling around the sofa. My face goes red through the green tinge of nausea. "I'm so sorry, Mum."

"You two owe me some sherry!"

"I'll nip to Sainsbury's today and pick up a bottle." Maybe I could pick up my dignity at the kiosk while I'm there.

Her stance softens, thank god. "It's not like you two to get rat-arsed this early in the month."

"Nic was all grouchy and sad, so I cheered her up with some good old karaoke." Beth has finally pulled herself together long enough to join the conversation. "And booze."

Mum's gaze lands back on me. "Why were you grouchy? Last I knew, you were going to see Aileen and Wally."

"I did." I say no more and hope Mum won't push it. No luck. Her eyebrow is in her hairline again. "Aileen was getting a bit much."

"Well, that's no surprise. About moving home or your love life?"

"The latter."

"You know she only does it out of love."

"And to be fair, sis, you do pick some wrong 'uns," Beth adds, fingering the knots out of her hair.

I glare at my smirking sister. "Butt out."

She rolls her eyes at me. "Nicole, you have the worst taste in women."

"Jesus, you sound like Tammy."

Beth points at me. "She's spot on."

Mum intervenes before I put Beth's head in the Christmas tree. "I understand she can be vexing, but was it that bad you needed to get pie-eyed with this one?" Mum juts her thumb at Beth, who is now wrapping herself up in the family Christmas blanket like a burrito, finally giving up on the rat's nest on her head. There's no rectifying that without a ton of conditioner.

"Oh, no, she got blotto because Niamh came into the pub with her tool of a girlfriend."

"Beth, will you shut up!" My head hurts.

Mum steps forward, putting her hand on my arm. "Did Pam—"

"Pat," I correct, although I love my mum even more for messing up her name on purpose.

"Right, that's it. Pat. Did she say something to upset you?"

"Not really. She just brought up our Christmas thing. Again."

"It's not difficult to understand," Beth mumbles from somewhere in her blanket cocoon.

Mum sighs. "Not everyone has the family we have, guys. For some, it might seem odd to spend as much time as we do together. Others wish they had what we have. Don't let anyone's questions or opinions upset you. Not like that. I can't afford fines from the council every time you get pissed off and decide to relocate council property."

I blanch. "You're getting fined?"

"Not this time. Not if you return those bloody cones."

Shaking off my hangover the best I can, I take the two steps needed to reach the couch and unfurl Beth. "Let's go." There's no way I'm letting Mum get into trouble over this. I can't believe I got so drunk over it, to be honest. Who Niamh spends her time with is none of my concern. I need to let the break-up with Steph stop messing with my emotions. Under normal circumstances, I wouldn't be giving any woman a second thought. Not when my time here is limited and precious.

There, it's decided. No more Niamh, other than strictly platonic and at a distance. Sorted.

"Before you both run off. I'm giving you a punishment." Her hands return to her hips again. She's in full-on mum mode.

"Mum, we're grown adults." Beth laughs.

"Yeah, you're sure acting like it," Mum retorts, daring us to argue. We do not. "Beth, you can head over to the tea shop later and take over the counter for the rest of the day. Give me and your sister a break." I silently laugh. Beth hates standing behind the counter. She's far too antsy to stay in one place for too long. "And Nic, you're going to take part in this year's calendar." Um, needle scratch. What?

"That's way more than a punishment, Mum!"

Throwing her hands in the air dramatically, Mum sighs deeply. "Fine, okay, I can't force you to do that. I'm hoping you will because you love me." She grins.

"Ah, the master manipulator strikes again." Beth laughs.

"Muum, come on." I'm thirty-seven. I swear I'm not this petulant child currently making an appearance.

"Please Nic, I'm desperate." God, she's even clamping her hands together in prayer.

"Why have you waited until now to ask?"

"I was going to ask you today anyway, but then you acted like a ruffian and I thought I'd use that to my advantage." She smiles.

"At least she's honest," Beth mumbles.

"You promised me I'd never have to do the calendar!" She's a bloody liar, liar, knickers on fire.

"I know, and I never asked, have I?"

"You're asking now."

"I'm begging now."

Bloody hell. Mum has volunteered at the local LGBTQIA+ centre since I came out. It was another way for her to show me support. Anyway, they started doing calendars a few years back. They sell them at the local Christmas market and at the tea shop.

When I first heard they were doing calendars, I made sure Mum and the rest of the group understood I would not—ever—participate. Female gay firefighter would've been on the top of their list, and I had to shut that down before it started. Mum promised me she'd never ask, and yet here we are.

"Why?"

"Amy Clever had to go home after her mum took a fall. She was our December!"

"You're telling me you haven't done the photo shoot yet?"

"No, it's set up for tomorrow. It's like herding cats trying to get it set up. There's always someone who can't make it."

"I've never understood why you don't shoot each month separately," Beth interjects, and she's not wrong. They could have the thing done months in advance if they wanted to.

"We like to have the Christmas party afterwards. It's nice."

Running a hand through my very bird's nest-style hair, I sigh. "And there is absolutely no one else who can help?"

"No one who's a firefighter."

"I'm not getting naked or showing my boobs!"

Beth almost chokes on her laughter. I'm so pleased my discomfort is entertaining.

"Nic, what kind of operation do you think we run?" Mum's voice is an octave higher than usual.

"The kind that likes to make money. I've seen the last three years, Mum!"

"No one was naked!"

"July 2023 left little to the imagination."

"I promise you won't be naked, love."

Famous last words.

"Where did you get Dad's boxers from?" I ask Beth, utterly bewildered how we dressed our traffic cones so neatly.

"How do you know I'm the one that got them?"

"Well, I wouldn't have."

Beth thinks for a minute before conceding. "Yeah, true. Your adventurous side doesn't really stretch to nicking underwear."

"God, they're heavier than they look." The traffic cones, not my dad's boxers. I groan like an old woman as I heave them off the ground. I need to do a workout. It's amazing how quickly the body loses its ability to work properly after a break from exercise.

"You're a buff firefighter. Suck it up."

"I'm carrying both, Beth!"

"Because you're a buff firefighter," she replies like I'm stupid.

It takes us a few minutes to drop them off at the council offices. Neither Beth nor I have any memory of where we picked the cones up from. Safe to say, the receptionist was less than impressed.

My day has *not* got off to the best start. Instead of enjoying a relaxing breakfast followed by a leisurely stroll down to the canal with Reggie and Liam, I'm hanging out my arse, coming to terms with the fact that I'm definitely going to be at least half-naked tomorrow in front of the members of Hebden Bridge's LGBTQIA+ committee.

Maybe I can cap the day off with a nice bath and one of Mum's hot chocolates. No sooner is the thought in my head than Liam comes crashing into the living room, buzzing about like a bee on steroids, announcing Niamh is on her way over to take him to the park.

A vague memory pulls my brain. Something to do with Niamh and... Ah, balls. "Liam?" Niamh's voice filters through from the front door.

"Nim!" Liam booms, barrelling through both Beth and me to get out of the room. "Nim, let's go!"

Yes, Nim, go. I really don't want an awkward encounter.

"Hold on, buddy. Is your mum in? I've been asked to drop something off for the calendar shoot tomorrow."

"Yeah, she's in the kitchen, cooking. She's still really mad at Nic and Beth."

"What did they do?" I can hear a hint of amusement in her voice.

"They got drunk on the trifle sherry and dressed up some orange and white cones."

I hear a snort of laughter that doesn't belong to Niamh. "Nice." Pat's voice follows. "Hey, buddy. I'm Pat."

"I'm Liam. Nim's best friend."

"Yeah, well, I'm her girlfriend."

Beth looks at me and rolls her eyes. I can't help but snicker quietly. Beth will automatically detest anyone that upsets me, which is sweet, but usually unfair on the person she targets. Although, in this instance, I'm not too bothered. Something about Pat rubs me the wrong way.

"I don't think you'll be her girlfriend forever," Liam replies, and I almost bite my tongue off. That dude really just says whatever's on his mind.

"And you might not be her best friend forever."

"Pat," Niamh chides quietly.

"What? He started it!"

And I'm going to finish it. Liam is extremely sensitive, especially when it comes to his relationships. If he thinks there is *any* chance he won't be Niamh's best friend forever, we're likely to have a really hard time with him.

Beth is right behind me as we enter the hallway. "Liam, don't worry mate, we know you'll be her best friend forever, right Beth?"

"Um, no doubt about it!" Beth smiles, nodding her enthusiasm. Liam shifts his gaze from me to Beth, looking for any hint of a lie.

"Of course, we will be best friends forever," Niamh adds, pulling Liam's hulking form into a hug. Liam lifts her from the ground, giving her a good squeeze while simultaneously glaring at Pat.

"Liam, put me down." Niamh laughs, finally breaking Liam's scowl. "Are you ready to go to the park?"

Liam looks from Niamh to Pat, then to me. I know he wants to ask me something he feels uncomfortable about. "Come on, bud, let's go find your other Batman jumper."

We head to his bedroom, which is all superheroes. Liam sits on his double bed and instantly fiddles with his fingers. "Nic."

"Yes, mate."

"I don't want to go to the park anymore."

"Okay, why not?"

He shrugs, even though we both know the reason. Liam's just too sweet to say it. "Just don't want to."

"That's fine. Do you want me to tell Nim?" He nods, his eyes on the floor.

I know how much he wants to go to the park with Niamh. It's the added extra that's the issue. If Pat hadn't acted like a jealous numpty, Liam would be on his way to have a good afternoon. There's only about an hour of light left, as is. I'm sure he thought Niamh would have been by a lot earlier. Frankly, I thought that too. But she's here now, and instead of Liam being excited, he's withdrawing.

"If you don't want to go to the park. Why don't we go and feed the ducks their dinner?"

"With Nim?"

"I think she's still going to hang out with Pat, buddy."

"Just us then," he states. Oh yeah, Pat has *not* done herself any favours.

"No problem. You stay here until I get back, okay?"

"Thanks, Nic."

Kissing him on his forehead, I head back downstairs. Niamh gives me a small smile. "Is he ready?"

"He's not feeling it anymore." I see her face fall and I hate it.

"Is he okay?"

"He will be."

"What's going on, babe?" Pat puts her arm around Niamh's shoulders.

"Liam isn't feeling well, so the park is off."

"Great, we dragged ourselves out in the sodding snow for nothing."

I lock my jaw before I say something I can't take back. Beth, on the other hand, has no such control.

"If I remember correctly, *Pat*, you invited yourself to Niamh and Liam's park time, so that's on you." Before Pat replies, Beth moves her gaze to Niamh. "Nice to see you, Nim. Come back soon. Maybe without the girlfriend." And then she turns and leaves. Awesome, it's just me, Niamh and Pat. Fabulous.

"Um, I should go too," I say lamely.

Niamh nods slowly, her eyes portraying her upset. "I'll call him later, okay?"

"Sure, he'll love to hear from you. Bye, Pat."

"Yeah, see ya," she replies, already halfway out the door. Niamh pauses for a few extra seconds before following.

Taking a deep breath, I physically shake off the last few minutes. I can hear Beth relaying what's just happened to

Mum, so I head back upstairs to Liam who I find peeking through his blinds.

"I don't think I like Nim's girlfriend," he mumbles, watching Niamh and Pat walk down the street.

"You don't know her, mate. Don't decide something on a first impression." *Wait until the second or third until you decide she's a twat.*

"Can we go feed the ducks now?"

"Sure. Get your big coat. It's freezing outside."

I can't recall a holiday that's started off so badly for me. Coming home for Christmas is my sanctuary, my time to de-stress, and yet, right now, I feel more wound up than ever.

Oh well, maybe an hour with the ducks and Liam will help. One can only hope.

# December 7th

Feeding the ducks didn't help. Mum's hot chocolate didn't help. Hell, Beth running out to the bakery this morning to buy my favourite breakfast pastry didn't help. I'm doomed.

The calendar shoot is mere hours away, and there is nothing I can do to get out of it. Worse, Mum is being tight-lipped with the details. I've asked repeatedly what I'm expected to wear and the only reply I get is a mumbling, incoherent sentence and a shrug before she suddenly remembers she has something to do. That doesn't bode well for me.

A week into my annual holiday and Operation Sleigh Bells is kaput. With all the other bloody drama going on, I've been sidetracked. By now I should have scouted the neighbourhood looking for possible bell mounting points. Tried again to sniff out conspirators next door and ransacked our parents' house in the slim hope that Mum left the bells somewhere easy to find them.

After this blasted calendar, I am refocusing all of my efforts. Instead of ruminating on my latest break-up and the reason Niamh dating Pat is giving me an ulcer, I will double down on unearthing Mum's secret. Come hell or high water I will prove victorious this year.

However, until that time, I have to concentrate on getting through today. Ugh, fuck my life. Thank god no one from my station is here to see my humiliation.

"Hello, bestie!"

Has my heart stopped? That sounded awfully like Tammy. But it can't be. She's back home making sure my house doesn't fall victim to Steph's vengeance. Turning from my spot by the kettle, I stare wide-eyed. I'm not hallucinating. Tammy is standing in my mum's kitchen with a wicked grin.

"No! What are you doing here?"

"Well, that's a fine way to greet me." She laughs.

"Tam. What. Are. You. Doing. Here?" If I grip my mug any harder, it'll break.

"A little birdie told me you're stepping in as Ms December. Is that right?"

"I'll fucking kill her," I seethe. Beth is about to get the biggest wedgie she's ever had. Slamming the mug on the worktop, I go to storm past Tammy, but she catches me by the waist, sending us into some weird dance-slash spin. I end up right back where I started.

"No, you will not. Well, not this second. Come here, I want a hug." Without moving a muscle, I let Tammy curl herself around my much taller frame. "Hug me back, you arse!"

Tutting, I dramatically throw my arms around her. "Is that better?"

"Yes."

"Tammy. Please don't tell me you travelled all this way just to watch me pose for this calendar."

"Of course not," she scoffs. "I came all this way to *record* you posing for this calendar. Future blackmail material, sweetie pie," she says whilst still hugging me.

"Now I'm going to kill you!"

"Stop." She laughs, batting me away from her. "You can't honestly say, if the shoe were on the other foot, you wouldn't be doing the same?"

"No! I can absolutely say I wouldn't, because I'm not the worst!"

"Bollocks. Nic, you made a video highlighting every fall, and face plant I took over a year's period. I'm still not sure how you got all that footage. *And* you showed it to the squad. Including the captain! Paybacks a bitch, my friend."

Damn it, I forgot about that. I even added Benny Hill music. Worth it!

"It's not my fault you're clumsy. And I didn't involve family members!"

"To be fair, Beth came to me! She was overly excited about it, actually. She's so vindictive sometimes. I love it."

"Tammy!" Mum squeals. "What on earth are you doing here, love?"

"Hi, Mrs R. I'm here to lend my support to the calendar shoot this afternoon."

"Oh, that's so nice of you. Want a sandwich?"

"Love one, thanks. Where's Liam?"

"War Room," I mumble. Tammy grins one last time and then leaves, presumably heading for the basement. She loves Liam like he's her own little brother.

"So why is Tammy really here?" Mum asks with a knowing smile.

"She's here because your youngest child is the devil!"

"Nicole Robinson!" The appalled tone would be believable if I couldn't see her silently laughing.

"Mother, she called Tammy specifically to get her here, to mock me."

"Tammy wouldn't do something like that unprovoked. Beth would, sure. But not Tam."

"Hence why she's the devil," I grumble. "I won't hear the last of this if my squad get a hold of the calendar! Or the video Tammy plans to make."

"Sweetheart, I wish you'd relax. It's just a picture. *And* think of all the good you're doing. The more we sell, the more we help your community. And as the proud mum who grew you, I think you should be happy to show off your bod a bit. You've got a cracking figure. And muscle. There are loads of eligible ladies out there who would love to get a piece."

Whining, I screw my face up in displeasure. "I don't want to talk to you about my body, Mum."

"Why not? We're open in this house!"

"Maybe a little too open."

"No such thing. Anyway, help me make these sarnies, and then we should head over to the centre."

As we construct gammon and mayonnaise sandwiches for the Robinson brood and Tammy, I silently plot my revenge. Beth is in for it now!

"Cooey," Aileen calls from the door. "Just came 'round to offer my best wishes. You'll do great, Nic."

"Does everyone know?"

"No point hiding it, sweetie. Most of Hebden will see the calendar," Mum replies, buttering more bread.

"At which point I will no longer be here! Couldn't you have kept quiet until then?"

"Oh, you're tetchy today," Aileen comments. Oh, how I love it when Mum and Aileen get together.

"I'm tetchy because I *do not* want to do this!"

"But you're helping me out, love. And you know how much I appreciate it!"

"No offence, Mum, but appreciation doesn't stop mortification."

"You've got a lovely body," Aileen adds.

"So we've established," I say through gritted teeth. I don't even know why I'm arguing.

"Nic, it will be over before you know it and you'll never have to do anything like it ever again. I promise. Now, please stop whingeing, eat your bloody sandwich, and put a smile on your face. This is supposed to be fun, and there are plenty of people who will show up today needing it to be fun. This is about as happy a Christmas as they will get."

Oouff, that one landed hard.

Nodding, feeling completely put in my place, I nibble on the crust of my sandwich, looking very much like the scolded child I am.

The rest of the family filters in, grabbing a bite and chatting among themselves. I keep myself to myself, knowing anything that comes out of my mouth right now will bring the mood down.

"Can we go now?" Liam asks the second he's finished his bag of crisps. I should have known this would turn into a full family affair.

"Yes, everyone get ready," Mum calls, whipping our plates from under us. Guess I'll finish lunch later.

"Is Dad coming?" I ask. I've seen him a grand total of two times since I've been home.

"He's already at the centre. He volunteered to help with the backdrops."

Super. Fan-fucking-tastic. Nothing like your old man seeing you in...well, I don't know what I'll be in, but I guarantee it's less than I'd like.

The snow is still falling as we make our way to the village. Normally we get a few inches in December, but this year the falling flakes are exceptionally early, and sticking around a lot longer. I do love it, though. Snow at Christmas adds to the magic, doesn't it?

Inside the Hebden LGBTQIA+ centre, people are buzzing about getting things set up. I see a few people who are clearly in the calendar too. One very buff guy with the best eyebrows I have ever seen is messing about with a pumpkin, so I'll guess he's Mr October.

"Nic, love, follow me." I trail begrudgingly behind Mum, making sure I give Beth a swift kick up the arse as I go by. She just laughs at me, making me more irritated.

I'm led into a small office area. There are costumes piled everywhere. My gaze zeroes in on mine. You can't miss it. Dropping my head, I prepare myself. "Who do they belong to?"

"Amy agreed to leave her uniform trousers here. The plan was for her to wear them with the suspenders covering her nipples. Helmet, of course, and boots."

"Right, let's back up a second. One, I will be wearing more than suspenders to cover my nipples. Bloody hell, Mum, Dad is out there. Plus a bunch of people I don't even know. You really thought I would—"

"No, I didn't, which is why we added a white tank top. We're replacing the helmet with a Santa hat. You'll be holding a fire extinguisher too."

"Okay, I can do that." This is so cringy.

"Lovely. The backdrop will be a winter wonderland. All you have to do is pose as a sexy firefighter! A few snaps of the camera, and boom, you're done. Easy peasy, love."

"Can I ask that I don't have an audience, please? I don't care if everyone else is okay with it. I'm really uncomfortable."

"Of course, sweetheart. No one here wants to make you feel like that."

Sucking in a deep breath, I nod. "Okay, do you need me to get changed now?"

"Let me check. Take a few minutes to calm yourself. I'll be back in five."

Five turned into twenty. By the time Mum came back, she looked a little frazzled.

"Sorry, love. You're scheduled last. We're going to get the shots done in month order. So far we're up to May. Why don't you come and watch? There are a few people here you know, and they'd love to see you, Nic."

"Yeah, why not?" She's right. I've been visiting the centre for as long as Mum's been volunteering. I know quite a few people, actually. I was clearly just having a meltdown earlier when I made the comment about a bunch of strangers watching me.

A backdrop is arranged in the main area. There are far fewer people than when we arrived. Ms May is in the middle of a pouty pose when Mum and I sneak in, hoping not to disturb anyone. I will not be pulling that face!

Mr June is next. He's in full rainbow attire, presumably because June is Pride month. He's flanked by two blow-up unicorns. The crew swiftly changes the backdrop from a spring vibe to party central. Mr June is a natural.

Everyone here is totally relaxed, making comments on how things can be improved, but not in a bitchy way. The volunteers all work well together, clearly wanting only the best for the calendar. It's really lovely to watch.

Once Mr June is done, the backdrop is once again changed, this time to a summer beach party. I see Mum shift nervously beside me, which is odd. That is until I see Niamh walk out in a bikini that can hardly be called clothing. Mother of Christ!

Now I understand Mum's aversion to any of my questions this morning. She knew Niamh was in the calendar and didn't want me to know until it was too late to pull out. There are a couple of things barrelling through my mind. One, is my...appreciation of Niamh so transparent that everybody can see it? Two, what the hell can I do to stop those appreciative thoughts? Because this will only end badly. For me, I'm guessing.

Niamh is Liam's best friend. She's dating Pat, and I'm leaving. Not to mention I'm seriously lacking in the ability-to-keep-a-woman department. What am I playing at? I promised to keep my thoughts platonic. But one glimpse at her in that bikini, and I can't repeat the things I'm thinking. How uncouth of me.

My face reddens, and I have to turn my head away slightly. However, when I do that, I look straight into Beth's eyes, which are staring right back at me, with a really annoying twinkle of amusement. God, I hate her sometimes.

I don't know where to look. Niamh is posing like a professional model. My eyes betray me and wander over her body. She's fit but still has soft edges. Her long hair shines under the lights. Her skin is pale, smooth looking and dotted with freckles. She's a delight to look at.

Squeezing my hands into fists, I will this to be over. Sure, I could leave, but how would that look? No, I just have to grin and bear it a little longer. Oh, look, that's a nice light fitting.

After a million years, Niamh is finally done and I can leave the room. Actually, I wait one minute exactly before making my escape. Don't want it to look too obvious, right?

Heading to the office, I burst into the space without a moment's thought. Right into Niamh, who is bare from the chest up, holding her bra in her hand, and a face that reflects my complete shock and embarrassment. Moreso, considering I'm just staring. The situation stretches on until we're locked in this superbly awkward staring contest.

Finally, Niamh places a hand on her hip and cocks her eyebrow at me. For whatever reason, that shakes me out of my stupor. I twirl around so fast I almost lose my balance. "I'm so sorry!"

"Did you need something, Nic?"

"Nope, I just came to get my costume."

"I'll be done in a second."

"Sure."

Silence. "Um...could you wait outside?"

"Fuck, yes, sorry." With one giant step, I exit and slam the door closed behind me. Standing in the corridor, I tap my forefinger to my forehead rhythmically. I was told it's some sort of meditation technique, and I sure as shit could do with some relaxation.

Still tapping away at my forehead, I hear the door open behind me. "The room is free now," Niamh says softly.

"Thanks." I can't look at her, not when her boobs are still vividly imprinted in my mind's eye. Shuffling past, I shut myself in the office and change. Nothing will stop my mind from running wild, so I'll try my best to distract myself.

Amy's gear fits pretty well. The tank top is super fitted, but I'm grateful I have it. There is no way my nips would have been covered by these suspenders. Fluffing out my hair, I add a thin layer of makeup. Might as well fully commit, I suppose.

Walking to the photoshoot area, I scan the room. No sign of Niamh. Phew. Ms November is just finishing up when Mum thrusts a Santa hat and fake fire extinguisher at me. It takes a second or two to get the hat just right.

"Okay, Nic," Brian, the photographer calls. "Ready when you are!"

I take a deep breath and get in position, doing my level best to channel Claudia Schiffer. She's literally the only model I remember. A few seconds in and I relax. Everyone is having a good time, and I have to admit it's quite funny. Until I see her! Niamh, in the corner, watching me intensely. The corner of her lip caught in her teeth.

# December 8th

I was the epitome of responsible last night. After the photoshoot wrapped up, everyone went a little crazy. The afterparty was wild. I'd learned my lesson and am now happily sitting in my parents' kitchen smiling widely at Beth, who looks horrific.

Beth, the wild child, certainly lived up to her namesake last night. To be fair, it's easy to see where she gets it from. Mum—who let loose alright, leaving me and Dad to chaperone Liam—spent most of the evening dancing and slamming back drinks with her youngest.

Even after a decent night's sleep, I am still replaying yesterday's events, aka Niamh O'Conner, watching me the way she did. As soon as my photos were done, I rushed to the office, changed my clothes, and snuck out the back door for a good hour. I'd rather run into ten house fires than deal with whatever the hell was happening there. I'm so confused.

One of my many girlfriends, Pria, read romance books like they were going out of fashion. She was obsessed. Her desire for me to live up to an idealistic and unreal character she had created in her mind caused several fights. I wasn't romantic enough. I didn't dote on her enough, and so on.

Anyway, I remember enough about those stories to know that the things I'm feeling for Niamh are a classic friends-to-lovers kinda trope. Or maybe Insta Love. Gross. But I know all that's crap. It's not real. No one walks into the love of their lives, and bam, they're all done navigating this cesspool of a thing we call dating.

I made the mistake of saying that to Pria once. Come to think of it, it's possible our substantial difference in opinion was the reason we split up and *not* my Christmas tradition with the family. Yes, that tracks.

So, back to my ridiculous feelings that are obviously a projection of some other trauma and not actual real romantic feelings I have towards Niamh. I can't get the look she was giving me out of my mind. It was no ordinary, "Hey, we're friends and I'm here to support you." look. Nope, it was full of... Dare I say it...desire? Lust? I felt that look down to my bones.

But what can or should I do about it? I've repeatedly mentioned she's Liam's mate and dating Pat. Plus, I'm leaving. All that was enough discouragement to do anything daft *before* I saw that look, and how it affected me. How it's still affecting me. I'll be honest, Niamh is my fantasy, all rolled up into one delightful package. But I've learned over the years, fantasies are usually never what they're cracked up to be.

I'm so tired of opening the little doors on my Christmas calendar. I'm tired of the fighting, of hurt feelings, and a general sense of not being what my partners need me to be for them. There is no reason to think that getting with Niamh, even for a holiday fling, would be any different.

Jesus, what am I going on about? It's totally presumptive to think Niamh would even want that with me. Looking at me like that doesn't mean squat.

"What are you thinking so hard about? You're making my headache worse."

"Serves you right." I have zero sympathy for my sister. This is karma at its finest. Tammy is yet to emerge from my room. No doubt she will be worse for wear as well.

"All right, fun police, back off. It's not my fault you were all boring."

"Boring, and not hung over."

"It's the price we pay to have fun, *Nic*!"

"That's possibly the saddest thing you've ever said, *Beth*."

"Girls, no bickering." Dad walks in with a newspaper in hand. Retirement suits him. He loved the police force, but the work took its toll.

"No bickering, Dad, just a discussion."

"Sure," he scoffs.

"What's your plan for today?" Mum, Beth, and Tammy aren't going far. Prime opportunity to get some father-daughter time in.

"I was going to head into the village for a walk along the canal. Want to come along? Liam can watch the barges."

"Love to. I'll get him ready. Leave this lot to their misery."

The weather is still in the minuses, with no indication it's going to warm up anytime soon. It really is unseasonably cold. Liam loves it. He feels like he's living at the North Pole. His words, not mine. I got a whole speech about it from him, on the way home last night.

"Liam, not too close to the edge, mate!" Dad calls. We tried to get him to learn how to swim again, but for whatever reason, he developed a fear of water after the accident. "So," he says to me. "Steph bit the bullet, huh?"

"Yup!"

"And how do you feel about that?"

Dad and I are quite close. He understands me and my introverted ways. I guess I get it from him. He can be a man of few words, but when he speaks, it's usually of importance.

Growing up, I always felt at ease talking to him. Mum too, but she definitely has the extrovert gene, which skipped me. My friends thought it strange I could talk to my dad about my period without embarrassment. Or that he'd buy me sanitary towels from the corner shop without batting an eyelid. I asked him once if he thought it was odd. He looked at me and said, "You're my kid. I helped make you. Why the bloody hell would I be embarrassed?" And that was that. I've told him about girlfriends, break-ups, even when I thought I'd gotten an STI. Nothing is off-limits.

The other difference between talking to him rather than Mum is that he rarely pushes his opinion. Mum, like most I think, pushes what she thinks is best for me. Dad listens and advises but leaves the decisions in my hands. I appreciate that.

"Honestly? I'm not cut up we're no longer together. It was exhausting trying to keep her happy."

"But?"

"But I thought I'd have settled down by now. I have a good job. Sure, it's not completely safe, but it's steady. I have a lot to offer, but it's never enough."

"Honey, you are enough. End of conversation."

"Tell them that." I laugh.

"No point. If they need telling, they're not right for you, Nic."

"Is it really that bizarre to spend December here?"

"Ah, another nonbeliever huh?" He smiles at me and I take a second just to take him in. I truly miss my parents when I'm away.

"You could say that."

"I'm no expert in love, Nic. I feel lucky to have held on to your mother for so long." He grins. "But I do know that the person you're meant to be with will never make you feel less than. They will be your partner in crime. Your best friend. If they aren't offering you that, walk away."

"All I seem to do is walk away. Or get walked away from."

"And that's how it should be, because none of those women were right."

I stop walking and look out at the water. It's so still. The frost paints such a beautiful picture hanging off the tree branches. Parts of the canal are frozen, but only thinly. The ducks manage to break it up as they go. "Do you think I should move home?"

"Do you want to?" Dad is standing next to me, appreciating the same picturesque scene, hands in pockets.

"I do, and I don't. Coming home makes me feel like I've failed, as stupid as that sounds."

"Gonna need a bit more than that, kid." I love he still calls me kid, even though I'm pushing middle age.

"Well, what will it look like? Things are a bit sad for me, so I come running home? I love the station, but I'd love any fire station."

"Tell me why you moved away."

"You know why, Dad. I needed to get out there. See some of the country."

"And you've done that. Do you still need that space?"

"No." I'm shocked at how easily the answer comes to me. I've mulled over the idea of moving back up North for a while now. I wouldn't want a house up the street from my parents. We're close, but even that would be too much. Maybe if I was closer, I could manage a relationship easier. Living a few minutes up the road would make the family tradition easier for whoever I'm with.

"Nicole. Moving closer to us would be wonderful, but only if that's what *you* want. Don't let anyone, not even your mother, force your hand."

I chuckle, because Dad knows better than anyone, Mum is a force of nature when she gets something lodged in her head. "Has she said anything about...Niamh?"

"Nothing other than she hopes you two get together and have beautiful babies."

"Oh my god, please tell me you're joking."

"Nope. Don't worry though. She knows how far she can push it before you have enough. She just wants you to be happy, and in her mind, that's with Niamh."

"Is Nim here?" Liam's voice booms, making me jump.

"No, buddy," I reply, hoping he didn't hear too much.

"Mum's right Nic, Nic. You should be Nim's girlfriend. Then you could both live close to me." Dad belly laughs and claps Liam on the back.

"Want a hot chocolate?" I'm shamelessly bribing him in the hopes he completely forgets this conversation.

We meander to the tea shop. Liam rushes in, almost taking the door off its hinges. Thankfully, everyone in town knows him and pays his exuberance no mind. "Mum, hot chocolate. Nic's paying."

Mum enters from the kitchen, where she is looking green. She didn't take into account her early morning when slamming back shots with Beth last night. "Liam darling, you don't shout, remember?"

"Sorry, Mum. But hot chocolate."

"Take a seat, and I'll get it for you." Liam doesn't need telling twice.

"Looking a bit peaky there, Mum." I grin.

"Oh, shut it, you. Go and sit down with your brother."

Laughing, I do as I'm told. We get into a very animated discussion about the merits of a superhero taking over from Santa if he ever wishes to retire. Our in-depth chat is interrupted by two humongous mugs of hot chocolate being placed on the table. I go to thank Mum but falter and freeze when I see it's actually Niamh.

"Nim!" Liam bellows. "Do you want to come 'round for dinner tonight?"

"Sure, your mum already asked me." Of course she did. "Hi, Nic."

"Hello."

"I didn't see you very much last night." *No, because I was avoiding you.*

"I had to take a breath after the photo shoot. And then I really didn't want another hangover, so I stuck to the fruit juice and the side of the dance floor."

"Ah, good call. I wasn't so fortuitous."

"A tad queasy?"

"Not anymore." She giggles. Actually giggles! "I had a plate of eggs and bacon this morning. That sorted me out." I bet Pat made her breakfast. Ugh.

"Sounds good. Beth hasn't been able to stomach anything so far. Maybe she'll be right by dinner."

She smiles at me, then looks to Liam, who is far too busy colouring in his napkin. Mum always has pencils at hand for him. Keeps him occupied. "I finish in ten minutes. Want to have a pint before dinner?"

"Um…" I see Mum looking over at us. Dad rolls his eyes and gently steers Mum out of sight. "Sure, okay. Will Pat be joining us?" *Please say no, please!*

"No, I thought it would be nice, just the two of us."

"Great, yeah, okay, sure." *Shut up!*

"Lovely. I'll come back over when I'm ready."

Fantastic, that leaves me ten whole minutes to freak out. Liam starts jabbering away again, but I can't invest this time. Dad arrives in the nick of time to stop Liam getting frustrated with my nonanswers. I know my eyes keep darting to the "employee's only" door, but I'm powerless to stop them. And then the door swings open and out steps Niamh, in her usual tight jeans and jumper, sans apron.

Standing on unsure legs, I zip up my coat and straighten my hood, for no reason. Can she tell I'm nervous? Would she understand the reason if she did? "Are you sure you want beer after last night? Um, and it's barely the afternoon."

"Hair of the Dog. I'll only have a half." We exit The Soggy Biscuit and silently head towards The Black Sheep. "Actually, why don't we go to my place? It's closer."

"Sure." What the hell else can I say?

A few minutes later, I'm not at all convinced Niamh's place is closer, because we passed the pub on the way. Does she want to get me alone? A few more minutes pass until we reach a set of gorgeous cottages.

"I'm this one," Niamh says over her shoulder as we enter the small garden via a very cute wooden gate.

"It's lovely."

"It's expensive." She laughs. "Renting around here is ridiculous." Hmm, that's something I need to consider. "But I love it. Two bedrooms, a nice bathroom, and open fireplace."

"Cosy!"

"Yes. And I can see the river from my back garden." She opens the door and heat hits me instantly. "Oh great, Peter started the fire for me."

"Peter?"

"My next door neighbour. He's a gem. When I work early, he pops over and gets the heat going for when I get home."

"That's really nice of him." Another Aileen and Wally, I think.

"Beer, wine, tea?" I watch as Niamh sheds her coat and boots. She's so effortlessly lovely.

"Tea, please. I'm keeping off the sauce for a few days."

"Mind if I have a glass of wine?"

"I know better than to keep an Irish lass from a drink," I jest.

She whirls 'round with fake outrage. "How very dare you...point out the truth." She winks. "Take a seat in the living room. It's bloody Baltic in the kitchen still."

Happy to take orders, I peruse the living room. There are a few art pieces, bespoke, if I had to guess. A picture of Niamh and her family and that's it. An old record player sits in the corner. Intrigued, I take a look at the vinyl in the player. Interesting. It's a Doo Wop album.

"I love old music," Niamh comments, handing me a cup of tea. "Nice to relax to it instead of the mindless bullshit on the telly."

"Agreed. You've got good taste."

"And you have impeccable biceps." Sorry. What? "Does it surprise you I said that?"

"Um, kind of." I chuckle nervously.

"But it's true. You've always been good to look at, but these ten years have done wonders."

Niamh is sitting quite comfortably on the sofa as I stand awkwardly by the record player, unsure what to say. And then I remember Pat. "Aren't you dating Pat?"

"Not exclusively. I told you that before."

"Yeah, but then you guys looked pretty 'together' the last two times we ran into each other."

"We're not exclusive, no matter how much Pat wants that. I'm not ready for serious."

I nod my head. "Okay, so..."

"Nic, can I be blunt?" Is this *not* her being blunt so far?

"Of course."

"I nearly swallowed my tongue when I saw you in your gear yesterday." I feel the heat bloom on my cheeks. "All I wanted to do was walk over and have you lift me over your shoulder." It's amazing how many women like that. "And, by the look you were giving me, I think you wouldn't have minded."

"No, I wouldn't have."

Niamh places her wine glass on the table and stalks over to me. I think my day is just about to get better.

# December 9th

It's 3:37 a.m., and I'm wide awake, staring at the ceiling. Niamh O'Conner's ceiling. That has lovely crown moulding. Weird thing to notice, especially in the position I'm in.

The sweat I worked up is still cooling on my skin. Niamh's soft snores are the only sounds penetrating the silence. My heart is beating fast, mostly from the acrobatic sex we've had over the past several hours. I'm talking dirty, dirty stuff. Niamh has some kink, and I was there for it!

Hours upon hours, with only a couple of water breaks. I thought I had a healthy amount of stamina, but I broke way before Niamh. The only reason I'm awake is because she let me have a nap at one point while she made dinner. And I'm pretty sure she only made me food because she could see I was flagging and needed to fuel me up again. As soon as my plate of Beef Chow Mein was finished, it was back to business.

For once, I didn't let my head override my heart. Well, it was more my libido, to be honest. The second Niamh put her hand on my face to trace the outline of my lips, I was gone. I remember it all in full HD, no, 4K. I wrapped my hand around her neck, pulling her forward into a kiss that was ferocious. After that, it was a blur of clothes flying, hands touching, and lips sucking.

She took me on the floor first. It was quick and dirty. I can't remember the last time I had a thorough fucking like that. I know I should be embarrassed how quickly I climaxed, but Niamh left me no time. She hauled me up, and I reciprocated on the sofa. We had a joint finish in the hallway, and then it was tit-for-tit for the rest of the night. Toys came out a couple of hours in. Niamh has an impressive collection. Then the silk ties. I've never tied anyone up before, but I'm adding it to my repertoire now.

Watching Niamh squirm on the bed, spread before me, unable to grab me, unable to close her legs as I took her hard and slow. I think it fundamentally changed me.

The last particular adventure we went on, the one that finally wore Niamh out, made me sweat and curse. She had me hold her up against the wall as I fucked her with a double-ended dildo. Then, as she was reaching climax, she ordered me to throw her on the bed and finish her from behind. My legs stopped working by the time she finally orgasmed and screamed the house down. I sincerely hope Peter—her neighbour—is deaf or has thick insulated walls. I also hope Niamh has some Ibuprofen gel on hand because my body is going to be screaming at me soon.

Now the fun is over, and my sex drive is back in the normal zone for the moment. My brain is kicking in again. I think this could have been a big mistake. Or was it? Bugger. Niamh mumbles something in her sleep, which is adorable. I watch her for a few minutes, trying to make a decision. Should I stay or should I go now? And yes, I did just sing that.

I've never snuck out before sunrise. I usually either get up and go straight after the act or stay for breakfast. Crap. I'm more of a relationship person than a one-night stand girl. "Sleep, Nic, please, your thoughts are way too loud."

"Sorry," I whisper, frozen in place. Niamh shuffles, and then I feel her breath on my neck. The room isn't cold, so I know it's her proximity that's causing goosebumps. Plus, my neck is a major erogenous zone so...

"Didn't I wear you out enough?" Her voice is a little scratchy with sleep, but her lovely accent is in full effect. God, it's even sexier when she's sleeping.

"I'm knackered. Believe me."

"Then what's wrong?" I feel her lift. Turning my head, I look into her eyes as she props herself up. "Do you want to go? Are you wondering how to leave without upsetting me?"

I've no idea if the thought upsets her or not. Her lovely face is blank. Neither happy nor sad.

"No, um...well, I didn't know if you wanted me gone before morning."

"Why would I?" She flops back down. "Go to sleep. I have crumpets for breakfast." Crumpets are my favourite.

The next time my eyes open, the sun blinds me temporarily. The space next to me is no longer occupied. Staggering from the bed, I search in vain for my clothes. I locate my knickers, and that's it. Spotting a bathrobe hung on the back of the bedroom door, I grab it, wrapping it around me. Padding through the cottage, I follow my nose. Crumpets are indeed on the menu.

Niamh is in cotton pyjama trousers and a tank top. The fire is already raging, heating the place nicely. Her hair is in a messy bun, and glasses. Glasses that make her look like a sexy, sleepy librarian. Is there anything this woman can't pull off? "Morning."

"Oh hey, right on time. Crumpets are served. Butter is on the counter and Marmite is in that cupboard." I follow her direction and take out the enormous pot of black goo. It's the food of the goddesses, I swear. Beth hates it with every fibre of her being. Which gives me an idea of how I get my revenge. Cue malevolent grin.

"Can I help with anything?" I feel like a bit of a spare part standing at the kitchen island with my pot of Marmite.

"Nope, sit. Here's your tea." How does she know I prefer tea with crumpets instead of my usual mug of java?

Once breakfast is set on the table, we quietly devour our food. I can't help but steal a few quick glances at her, worrying if she's feeling as awkward as me. Suddenly, she bursts out laughing.

"You really don't do this often, huh?"

"This?"

"Casual sex. One-night stands. Nic, you look petrified."

Of course, I choke on my crumpet. Shaking my head, I manage to swallow it with a gulp of tea. "No, I don't, and I'm not sure of the etiquette."

"Etiquette." She grins. "My, my."

"Alright, shut up." I smile through my blush.

"I don't want you to feel uncomfortable around me, Nic. Last night was wonderful. I like a woman who can keep up."

Ugh, my thoughts stray to Pat. Can she keep up?

"I enjoyed it too." That's a major understatement. I've never had sex like it.

"So, let's not get in our heads about it. I'm attracted to you. I have been for a very long time. If this happens again, I'm okay with that."

"But...um, what about Pat?"

She rolls her eyes. "I feel like I'm on repeat. We aren't exclusive. My last relationship really took it out of me. I'm not in a place for serious just yet. So I have fun. If you're okay with that, I want to have fun with you."

I nod again. Really, I'm about as smooth as gravel. "Okay."

"More words, Nic."

"Yes, I'd like to have more fun with you. As long as we both stay on the same page. It's just casual. And...um, Liam doesn't know. I'm not sure how he'd take it."

"Agreed. Same with Beth, because—"

"She's the devil," I add, causing Niamh to laugh.

"I was going to say a gossip."

"That too."

"Won't they notice you stayed out last night?"

Yes, they absolutely will, and I'm not convinced I'm going to be able to pull off a lie. Mum will see straight through me. Especially considering she invited Niamh for dinner and neither of us turned up. "It'll be fine." Niamh raises both eyebrows in a, "You're kidding, right?" kind of way.

"If you say so. What have you planned for today?"

Polishing off the rest of my breakfast, I sigh. "I'm way behind on Operation Sleigh Bells."

"What's on the list?"

"I'm supposed to have swept the house by now."

She cocks her head to one side. "Do you do that every year?"

"Yup."

"Do you search the house multiple times?"

Frowning, I shake my head. "No point."

"But what if your mum simply moves the bells from place to place, knowing that once you've searched an area, you don't return?"

"Um..."

"She's not daft enough to keep them in one spot the whole time."

"Well, now I just feel stupid."

"Yeah, you kind of look it too." She grins. I throw crumbs at her in protest.

"But how would she find the time? I know Mum thinks our yearly search is childish—"

"She loves it, and I'd bet my wages she finds it highly entertaining to mess with you."

No doubt. I just assumed she let us get on with it each year, keeping an eye from the sidelines. Possibly recruiting the neighbours to help out if necessary. But what if Niamh's right? Mum could be feigning disinterest in our project and secretly be fucking with us.

But, she has the tea shop, which takes up a lot of her time. Sure there's Dad. Us kids have always known he's involved somehow. I gasp. What if this is so much bigger than we realise? "Your eyes have gone really wide."

"I need to get back to HQ. We need a meeting."

"Can I tag along?"

"Absolutely. I'll call Beth."

"Well, look what the Irish cat dragged in!"

"I take it I'm the cat in this situation," Niamh responds easily to Beth.

"Yes, you are. Where, may I ask, did you two disappear to last night?"

I sink into the couch. It's completely battered from years of abuse at the hands of three kids. "Not that it's any of your business, but we had a few drinks and it got late, so I stayed at Niamh's place."

"Uh, huh. And during those drinks did you decide to take self-defence class that got out of hand?"

I scoff. "What are you banging on about?" That was the wrong move. I immediately see the second Beth knows I walked into her trap.

"Well, with what looks like a hand mark on Niamh's neck and a substantial bruise that could also be a hickey on yours. It got me wondering. The bar must have been rowdy."

My eyes fly straight to Niamh's neck, and the memory of her asking me to hold her by the throat as I fucked her comes to mind. I scour her skin. And yes, that's when I see a faint outline of my hand.

I'll be honest. My first reaction is to march over and soothe her skin with my tongue. Did I hurt her? I swear I didn't put any pressure into the hold, but I must have. Our eyes meet and I see her trying to reassure me, but it doesn't work.

Beth snickers, like the irritating little arsehole sister she is. "Wait until I tell Mum."

"Beth!" I snap, not in the mood. "You'll say nothing to Mum."

"And why's that?"

"Cyprus."

She pales, and I know I've won. It's the only thing I have to rein her in. I'm a vault with people's secrets, but I'm not above using them as leverage when needed. Where Beth is concerned, that is.

"Alright, I was only kidding," she mutters, going red. Niamh is looking between us, intrigued. "But you did, didn't you?" Beth quickly adds on. "You did it!"

I'm saved by my wonderful brother barrelling down the stairs, still in his Superman pj's. "I brought snacks," he calls excitedly. "Nim, I'm so excited you're in the club now." We all smile.

"Me too. It's taken me twenty years to get here." She laughs, but I glean a sliver of truth behind her words. Has Niamh always wanted to be a bigger part of this?

Realising she isn't getting any salacious gossip out of us, Beth turns to the matter at hand. "So, what's with the emergency meeting?"

"Niamh pointed something out, that really, we're stupid not to have figured out before."

"And what's that?" Beth is picking her cuticles, which drives me nuts.

"Mum has been playing us."

"What do you mean, Nic?" Liam asks through a mouth full of mini doughnuts.

"Think about it. This is our thing, right? Every year, we try our best to find those bells. And every year Mum laughs at us but seemingly leaves us to it."

"Yeah, and?"

"And she's not leaving anything. Niamh asked me if we search the house multiple times, to which I said no. I think you two would agree that once we've searched an area we move on, right?"

"Yeah," Beth answers, clearly intrigued.

"And that's been fine when we thought Mum couldn't care less. Just her three nutty kids keeping up this tradition. But what if she's still very much involved? What if she is actively hiding the bells? Moving them from place to place, knowing we won't search again. Let's be honest, it's not like we change up our searching M.O. each year."

"That's because there's only so many places we can look," Beth replies, sitting forward.

"Exactly. Mum knows we stick to our plans, so it's easy for her to keep the bells hidden—"

"For Santa," Niamh interjects, her eyes slipping to Liam.

"Absolutely, she's his best worker!" I say emphatically. Liam's eyes light up.

"Okay, I see where you're going. How do we catch her out then?"

"By doing things randomly. Changing it up."

"We can sweep the house, but then a few days later do it again? Same with Aileen and Wally's."

"And we have a new club member," Liam pipes up. "Nim can search the tea shop and listen in. Maybe she will catch Mum talking to Santa?"

"I can do that." Niamh nods enthusiastically, clearly enjoying herself.

"But we need to keep Mum in the dark. Stop making it so obvious what we're doing."

"Tough call, sis," Beth adds. "She's like a hawk. Plus, she'll know something is up if we change *too* much. We need to keep up the ruse."

"Okay, so we need to maintain the norm while simultaneously changing everything we usually do."

Beth shivers. "I can feel it, Nic. This is the year."

I stand and high-five her. Niamh chuckles. Liam claps and squeals in excitement.

"Hands in, team," I say. Three other hands land on mine. "This is the year. Everyone with me?" There's a collective shout of "hell yeah." "On the count of three. One... Two... Three...go Team Sleigh Bells."

# December 10th

I didn't even know Tammy was still here, if I'm being honest. But that's definitely her seemingly lifeless body strewn across my bed. Taking the golden opportunity to add some material to my blackmail file, I snap a couple of pictures. The slobber really adds to the effect. Let's see how quick she is to show the calendar footage to the squad now.

She can't have been in bed for two days, right? But the smell sure suggests that. Whipping the covers back, I wait for a shriek, but Tammy snores on. A firmer touch is needed, which I'm quite happy about. I still haven't forgiven her for colluding with Beth. Especially if I find out Steph egged my house or something while Tammy was here mocking me.

Shoeing off my trusty elf slippers, I climb onto the bed, planting both feet on either side of Tammy's torso. With a huge amount of satisfaction, I launch myself into the air. Tammy's body bounces as I land, but will I stop? No way. She deserves multiple bounces.

Finally, getting the shriek I deserve, I give one final jump before hopping off the bed. Tammy is clutching her chest, eyes wide. "What the bloody fucking hell?"

"Morning, sunshine!" My grin is obnoxious.

"You just wait, Nicole Robinson! I'm going to murder you in your sleep."

"Tad much, Tam. Come on, the day's wasting."

She growls at me, her eyebrows pinched. I'd be more intimidated if her hair wasn't so ridiculous. "I'm posting the calendar footage all over the internet."

Shrugging, I smile. "Go for it."

Having the upper hand over my best friend doesn't happen very often, so I shall bask in the moment. Her eyes narrow as she tries to suss out why I'm being so chill. "What did you do?"

"Oh, nothing... Maybe snapped myself a little insurance, is all."

"You..." She grits her teeth. Breathing deeply through her nose, Tammy sticks out her hand. "Truce?"

"Truce." We shake on it. "Now, are you really only just getting out of bed since the calendar party?"

Tammy nods her head solemnly. "I'm officially in the two-day hangover part of my life. I thought I was dying yesterday."

"You did go pretty hard on the eggnog."

"Please don't say that word. It's ruined for me."

"Shit, did it make a reappearance?"

"I think lunch from last week made an encore. Never again Nic, I swear it."

Snorting, I shake my head. "Tammy, you have about four different Christmas parties to attend this month. You're telling me it'll be a dry Christmas?"

"Yes. I think I pickled my liver."

Walking over to Tammy's bag, I rifle through it until I find a hairbrush. Seriously, it's disturbing me seeing her in such a mess. "Here, you'll probably need to condition your hair several times first, but honey, you gotta sort that out," I say, pointing. "And you stink."

"Yeah, alright."

"Meet you downstairs. We can go for a walk, grab a tea at the shop. You need some fresh air."

While Tammy is in the bathroom, I take the opportunity to do my first bit of snooping. Mum is at work. Dad, Beth, and Liam are shopping at Sainsbury's, so this is the best time to look for the bells.

Over the years, I have searched this house plenty. Not just for the sleigh bells, but for presents, Mum's hidden sherry stash, and Beth's lost retainer. I've looked in every nook and cranny of the place. To be honest, I'm not sure what I expect to be different this year. Mum knows we're going to look, and as hopeful as I am that we can trip her up by searching several times. I just think she's too clever. It's like a mum superpower.

I'll leave my parents' room until last. I'm still not over the search of 2020. At thirty-three, I did not need to find my parents' play drawer, if you catch my drift. I still shudder at the contents. I couldn't look either of them in the eye for quite a while.

Liam's room takes me a few seconds to sweep. Mum would never risk him finding the bells, but I look just in case. Beth's room is a pigsty. She's seriously a hot mess. But her room has a built-in deep wardrobe we used to play in the back when we were kids. There are still drawings on the wall. Hieroglyphics, if memory serves. We thought ourselves a regular trio of treasure hunters, and of course we always ended up in Egypt trying to decipher ancient text.

After rifling through the closet for a few minutes, I give up. Even if Mum did smuggle the bells in here, I'd never find them under all Beth's crap. How Ted copes is beyond me. The man is a saint. Maybe it's time I spoke to Mum about clearing some of our childhood junk out. I highly doubt Beth's four Tamagotchis need to be stored any longer. Or her school uniform from twenty years ago. Jesus, it's like an episode of *Hoarders*.

The bathroom door clunks shut and Tammy shuffles by Beth's open door. She pauses, looks at me and the mess, then carries on. Tam has been around long enough to know what I'm doing. The hairdryer comes to life, giving me roughly two centuries to search the house. Tammy and her haircare routine is the bane of my life. I've tried to get her to speed up the process, but after I had countless hairbrushes, combs, and even a hairdryer itself launched at me, I knew it was a losing battle.

Miraculously, ten minutes later Tammy sweeps into the kitchen, where I'm currently wedged under the kitchen sink cupboard. They really need to get these pipes refitted.

"So, can you put your builder's arse away and make me coffee?" Tammy calls.

"Tam, the kettle is right there," I reply, pointing blindly, my head still firmly focused on finding hidey holes. Although, it would make one hell of a racket if Mum did hide the bells here. It's a tight space and I'm sure they'd clang when removed. No, this is another dead end.

Tammy is still sitting at the table when I emerge, covered in cobwebs. The kettle is *not* boiling. Rolling my eyes, I prepare two mugs of instant coffee. "Feeling better?" I ask, sitting on the opposite side of the table.

"A bit. Maybe I got food poisoning or something."

Snorting, I shake my head. "No, you had a case of way too much alcohol. Don't try to blame the food for it. You and Mum were in rare form."

Tammy's head hits the table with a *thunk*. "Ugh, stupid Tammy," she mumbles.

My shoulders shake with silent laughter. She's such a drama queen and I love it. "Ah, come on, get that down your neck and we'll get out of here. We have a few things to discuss, missy."

Life slowly starts to seep back into my best friend as we stroll through the snow-blanketed streets. The weather forecasts another three days of snow starting tonight. I need to make a mental note to check Mum and Dad's emergency supplies. It's a running joke that the U.K. can't handle bad weather. We get a few inches of snow and the whole country shuts down. However, the weather up North is no joke. The past few years have seen the winters turn brutal. I put together a home emergency kit two years ago and took my parents through it. Liam thought it was amazing and openly stated he wanted them to get snowed in.

The kit is simply a bag with a battery-operated torch (plus spares), a radio (batteries included), a phone charger, a first aid pouch, and a few days' worth of dehydrated food. I also included loo roll—because we all remember what happened when people thought toilet roll might become hard to buy during the COVID craziness. A couple of blankets are in there too, although they obviously have duvets and such in the house. I was just being extra cautious.

There's also a multi-tool, a whistle, and a folding shovel for snow. It's unlikely they'd ever get snowed in, but I'm not around all the time, so I want to make sure they're prepared. Each room has a fire extinguisher, and the upstairs bedrooms have fire ladders that can be thrown out the window.

Beth takes the piss out of me for being "Way too serious about safety." I'd rather be over the top than negligent. I sometimes think Beth forgets the shit I've seen on the job.

"Hey, earth to Nic."

"What? Sorry, I was just making a note to check something."

"So, are we going to get to the whole 'we need to talk, missy' section of the walk or what?"

I laugh. "Yes. Am I going to get home to find my windows caved in? You were supposed to be on lookout for Steph."

"And I was," Tammy begins. "The crazy fucker marched up your steps the very next day with a can of spray paint."

My hands reflexively go to my temples. "Jesus Christ!"

"Uh huh. But don't worry, I was there with my phone pointing in her face. I told her I was recording everything, and that you would report her if she stepped foot on the property again."

"Wow, okay, nice one."

"I also said all the neighbours were on neighbourhood watch, so..."

"Do you think it worked?"

Tammy tuts. "Nic, I told you she was fucking barmy from the start. But she's not stupid. A criminal record would see her without a job. The worst she'll do now is smear your name in the local lesbian community."

"Oh, that's all, huh?"

"Yeah, and so what? You'll still get pussy. All you gotta say are two words and you'll be neck deep in minge."

"Two words?"

"Lesbian firefighter. Huh, is that three words?"

We round the corner to The Soggy Biscuit. My heart does a little cartwheel when I spot Niamh through the window. Shit, I need to either tell Tammy I've had acrobatic sex with the Irish delight or try to keep her as far away from Niamh as possible. The thing is, Tammy inevitably finds shit out, and it will be so much worse if she doesn't hear it from me. "Okay, listen before we go in. I need to tell you something."

Pulling her to the bench on the opposite side of the street, we sit. Tammy is full of intrigue. "What did you do?"

"Okay, so... Right..."

"You shagged someone!"

"What? How in the hell do you know that?"

"Because, Nicole Robinson, you're stuttering as if a pretty woman just spoke to you. And even though I'm fucking gorgeous, you don't stutter around me. Therefore, you thought of the woman who did make you stutter. Adding that to the blush creeping up your neck, I conclude you had sex!"

It scares me how she does that. "Okay, yes, I had sex. Um, with Niamh."

"Whoop, yeah, you did, you big lezzy muff muncher!"

"Oh my god, stop." I laugh, tugging her arms from the sky back to her sides. "Look, Liam can't find out, okay? You know what he gets like where Nim is concerned."

Tammy nods. "Roger that. Keep schtum on the sex talk."

"And can you not embarrass me in front of her? Like, just give me a break this time."

She narrows her calculating eyes. "Only if you delete whatever awful picture you took of me this morning."

Ugh, well, that's no fun. "Done!"

"In front of me, Nic. I wasn't born yesterday."

Making a big show of taking my phone out, scrolling to the picture and deleting it, I give her a well-timed "Happy now?" smirk.

"Fine, I'll be super nice and not mock you. Now, can we go inside? I'm colder than a witch's tit."

We head indoors and grab the only open table. Niamh really has done a fantastic job of driving more business to the tea shop. Mum waves to us as we settle down. I don't even need to order; she knows why I'm here. Niamh backs out of the swinging doors that lead to the shop kitchen. She's laden down with a tray full of cakes and tea. My eyes obviously fall to her arse. I don't feel creepy now. I've had my hands on those delicious cheeks.

"I don't even want to know what that look means, but can you stop it? I want to enjoy my hot chocolate without watching you get all hot under the collar."

I slowly sweep my eyes back to Tammy. "Huh?"

"Ugh, gross. Nic, I said I wouldn't embarrass you, but if you don't put your eyes back in your head, I'm going to have no choice, mate. It's like a best friend prerogative, and your dribbling is making it way too hard to resist."

Right, yes, I need to get a grip on myself. It's tough though. Now I know we could be having sex again, at any time, it's like my libido is on a runaway train. I can't stop thinking about Niamh. Pat walking into the shop sure as shit extinguishes that low-set fire though. Fuck, for a few glorious seconds I forgot about her. I watch her make a beeline for Niamh.

Not wanting to witness whatever vomit-inducing thing Pat is about to do, I turn to Tammy, who is watching me closely. "Who. Is. That?" she asks, her brow arching. She's looking over my shoulder.

"That would be Pat. She's seeing Niamh. Casually."

"That's casual?" she asks, and I can't help but peek over my shoulder. Fucking hell, this is a place of business. Pat is all but mauling Niamh.

Turning back 'round, I sigh. "Apparently."

"Jesus. Okay, so do we hate Pat?"

I chuckle. "You don't know her, so no, you don't hate her." Tammy is similar to Beth in a lot of ways. Ready to hate the world at my request. "I don't hate her, but she's not my favourite."

"Right. I'll reserve judgement then. Oh, um, I need to talk to you...about something."

Tammy is nervous, which is super weird. "Are you okay?"

"Um, well yes. There was another reason I came to see you."

"Which is." I gesture for her to continue, but she just bites her lip. "Hey," I say, reaching over and taking her hand. "Sweetie, you can tell me anything."

"I'm leaving the service. I quit."

What in the world?

# December 11th

Tammy's news is either a Christmas miracle or a Christmas nightmare. Unfortunately for me, I couldn't keep my stupid, judgemental mouth shut long enough to find out. This whole staring at the ceiling malarky is already becoming repetitive. I usually sleep like a baby when I come home, but this year, not so much. I keep replaying Tammy's heartbroken face as I laid into her. Stupid arsehole. She's my best friend. My *pregnant* best friend. The second the words came out of her mouth I berated her for getting blackout drunk the other night.

Turning my head, I look at the clock—5:15 a.m. I've probably had all of three hours sleep. After Tammy broke down in uncontrollable sobs, Mum rushed over and shooed me away. I felt completely shitty but didn't leave. It took Mum a good ten minutes to calm Tammy down, by which time I realised how badly I'd fucked up the situation.

Looking utterly devastated, Tammy allowed Mum to take her home. I followed behind with my head down in shame. Back at the house, Beth, Liam, and Dad all rushed over to see what the drama was, only to have Mum practically growl at us all.

We retreated to the kitchen, where Beth tried to get the gossip out of me, but I kept my lips tightly sealed. The only thing I wanted to do was make things right with Tammy.

I never got the chance. Tammy escaped to my room and stayed there for the rest of the day. I went to knock on the door several times but Mum simply shook her head. Not knowing what to do with myself, I walked around Hebden for a few hours until it was late enough that I could hide away in the War Room. Tammy could have my bed for as long as she needed.

And that's where I am. On the sofa in the War Room, berating myself for being such a fucking dumbass. Tammy is amazing, and she's been through some shit. Lost both her parents in an avalanche when she was eighteen. No other siblings, and only one surviving grandparent. That's why she moved to join my station when her wanker husband left. She only has me, and I behaved like such a moron when she needed me to be her best friend. Lord knows she's done enough for me.

My stomach is alive with angry frogs. I can't lay here any longer without talking to Tammy. She'll hate me even more for waking her up, but I have to. Mum will be up shortly, so I'll sneak upstairs now.

Avoiding the squeaky step, I climb to the landing, taking a few deep breaths. I am ready to prostrate myself at her feet until she forgives me. My bedroom is dark and smells of tears, if that's possible. Tammy is huddled up in the foetal position at the edge of the bed. Tip toeing over, I watch her sleeping. She looks so peaceful. Shaking away my guilt, I sit on the bed and gently nudge her shoulder. She grumbles several times before her eyelids flutter open. There's just enough light in the room to see her eyes lock onto me. I can see the mix of hurt and anger etched across her face.

"Hey, can we talk?" I whisper. She lays silent. Tammy is excellent at the cold shoulder. However, I know her weakness. Clearing my throat I begin to sing *Wham Last Christmas*. I even stand up and start to dance. Let the record show, I suck at dancing.

It's just at the start of the second verse she finally breaks, her head shaking and a quiet chuckle leaves her throat. It's raspy, so I know she's been crying a lot.

"Okay, no need to deafen me. Shut up and sit down."

Sinking on the bed, I take her hands the moment she's finished adjusting herself against the headboard. "Tam, I'm so sorry. I'm a fucking idiot."

"Yes, you are."

"Please forgive me." The frogs are leaping about double time as I watch her watch me.

She sighs. "You know I will."

I draw her in for a bone-crushing hug. "I love you, Tam. I'm here, for whatever you need, okay? Will...will you tell me about it now?" A tear escapes one eye. I reach forward and brush it away.

"Not much to say. I had a one-night stand that resulted in a baby."

"Tammy."

She sniffs. "What am I going to do, Nic?"

"Do...do you want the baby? Um, how far along are you?"

"Nine weeks yesterday. I think I've just been in shock. I should have told you earlier, but I couldn't form the words, Nic. I'm in no fit state to be a bloody mum, but I'm not sure I can have an abortion either."

This is way out of my comfort zone. I'm sure my mum, or even Beth, would be better suited for this discussion, but they're not here, and Tammy is my bestie, so I need to buck up. "Why don't you think you'll be a good mum?"

Tammy scoffs. "I'm alone, Nic. I have no family. I can't be a firefighter and have a baby. Let's be honest, I've been a wreck after twat face left. What the hell do I know about raising a kid?"

I shuffle a little closer and grip her hands harder. "You have family. Right here. You know that. And I'm guessing that most new parents haven't got the first bloody clue what to do with a baby. I know you'd be a good mum, if that's what you want. Whatever you choose, I'll support you."

"I... I couldn't tell your mum. I felt so ashamed. I just thought if I pretended it wasn't happening, I didn't have to deal with it. And I didn't drink the other night. I just made out like I did. I wasn't ready to tell you, and I knew you'd wonder why I wasn't drinking, so I pretended I did.

The fact is, I have been sick, but it's morning sickness rather than alcohol poisoning."

Well, don't I feel like a Grade A arsehole. "You have nothing to be ashamed about. Do you want me to tell her? I think she's going to grill me, anyway." Tammy nods her head and then yawns. "Okay, sweetie. Get some more sleep and I'll talk to her. I love you, Tam."

"Love you too, Nic, even if you are a douche canoe at times."

That's fair. I wait until she's settled back down before creeping out of the room. Muted clanks come from the kitchen. Mum's awake. Well, no time like the present. I'm pretty sure she's going to try to ground me or something for being so insensitive.

Sure enough, Mum's sat at the kitchen table in her dressing gown slurping on a big mug of coffee. "You're up early, love."

"Yeah, I couldn't sleep."

"That to do with Tammy, by any chance?"

I nod. "I messed up, Mum. Tammy told me something, and I completely flew off the handle on her."

"Am I allowed to know what the big secret is?" Placing her mug on the table she turns to give me her full attention.

"She's pregnant, and instead of listening, I chewed her out for drinking. Even though she didn't actually drink at the party. It was all fake to hide her news."

"Not your best moment, Nicole." Ugh, the full-name treatment.

"I know. I think I was just gobsmacked and reacted poorly."

"Have you spoken to her?"

"Just. I woke her up. I couldn't stand feeling so shitty a second longer. God Mum, I feel like that's the theme of my life at the moment. Feeling shitty and buggering up."

"No need to go down that path, love. You apologised, right?"

"Of course."

"So that's a start. Did she say what she wants to do?"

"I don't think she knows. She's terrified, and I get it. But whatever she wants, I'll be there. She can move in with me if she wants. I'll help with the little one."

"Have you offered that to her?"

"No, she was tired, so I sent her back to sleep. We'll talk more later."

Mum studies me for a few moments. "You're restless, Nic. I've not seen you like this since you decided to move away. What's going on?"

Running a hand through my hair, I look everywhere but at Mum. "I dunno," I mumble. I *am* thirty-seven, I swear.

"Wow, I just had a flashback of your teen years!"

Grinning, I lean my elbows on the table and rest my face in my hands. "I'm approaching forty. I have a job I love, but my love life is just a disaster, and I don't know, I feel unsettled."

"Why haven't you spoken to me?"

Ugh, more guilt. I know I can talk to my parents about anything, but confessing to my mum that I miss home is stupid.

"Because it feels daft, Mum."

"What does? Nic, what do you want? What change do you think you need?"

Scratching the back of my neck, I huff. "I've considered moving back to Hebden Bridge."

Mum looks confused as hell. "Why the bloody hell wouldn't you tell me that?"

"Because if I come home, I'm failing more!" I didn't mean to blurt that out.

"Sorry, love. You're going to have to spell that one out, because I don't understand your logic at all."

"I moved away to make something of myself. Or at least prove I could be independent. And what, things get a little tough, so I come running back home."

Mum shakes her head. "Honey, I don't know where you got the idea that you needed to move away to prove yourself. There is nothing wrong with being happy in the place where you grew up."

I'd quite like some of Mum's outrageously strong eggnog right now. "I just... Beth and Liam both excelled, you know. Beth was a wiz at science, Liam should have been a football star. I always feel like I'm playing catch-up. I'm a firefighter, and that's my dream job, but even that was hard to fit into."

"Nicole. Beth spent many a night crying, stressed, and needing comfort. She's all bravado, you know that. As for Liam, he may have become a footballer, but let's be honest, before the accident, he was a lazy shit. Far too happy to let you do things for him. The same goes for Beth. I love you three kids equally, but my god, that pair put all the burden on you, and you took it. That's the reason they seemed to skate through life, sweetheart. Because they handed over all responsibility to you."

"So, you're saying I should murder my siblings? That's what I'm hearing." I get a playful clip 'round the ear.

"I'm saying you're a caretaker. You naturally want to make sure everyone is okay. Of course you make an exceptional firefighter. You're literally playing to all your strengths. So, just because your love life isn't quite where you want it, doesn't mean you're failing. Wanting to be closer to the people you love doesn't mean you're failing. If you don't think Beth will be on the first train home when she's pregnant, you're delusional. You're not the only one who enjoys the comfort of home. And I love that. I always wanted you kids to feel you could come home, or at least be close to home whenever you like. Hebden is home. That's not something you need to fight, love."

This is a lot of self-reflecting and analysing to be doing at six in the morning. I need time to mull it all over and decide if what I'm feeling is a true need to change, and possibly move or just the unfortunate after-effects of a shitty few days.

"I'm going to get ready for work. Don't forget we're building gingerbread houses this afternoon. I invited Niamh." The sparkle in her eyes is as subtle as shit in a swimming pool. But the mention of Niamh has done a good job of distracting me. I'm one thousand percent sure my face is flushing and my eagle-eyed mother has picked up on it. Excusing myself rather hastily, I slip back to the War Room, and settle back on the sofa.

The power nap I managed to snag has done me a world of good. It's now 10:00 a.m. and I'm freshly showered and making breakfast for Tammy, who I heard moving about roughly ten minutes ago. Sure enough, she pads into the kitchen in her Santa gnome onesie. I'm happy she takes the sanctity of Robinson tradition as seriously as the rest of us.

The chat with Mum and a little time alone has given me a clear picture that, yes, I'm ready for a change. I'm not quite at the deciding stage yet, but I'm going to stop resisting it. First, though, I want to make sure Tammy is okay. I hate the idea of her going home alone, so I'm going to see if I can get her to stay. "Morning, sunshine."

"Mmm, are you cooking eggs?"

"Yup, your favourite. Scrambled."

Her face goes green and then she rushes to the downstairs loo. Throwing every window in the kitchen open, I dispense the eggs in the bin. It doesn't take a genius to figure Tammy's aversion to her favourite breakfast is due to morning sickness. And then I realise that pregnant people shouldn't have eggs, anyway. Crap, I'm going to need to read up and learn some stuff.

"Sorry." I wince when she reemerges.

"It's fine. The sickness is getting less nowadays."

"Cereal? Toast? Orange Juice?"

"Just toast, please." We fall silent as I make her food. She looks shattered.

"I want you to stay," I blurt out the second her plated buttery toast lands on the table.

"Nic, I'm too tired to work out what you're banging on about."

"Stay here until Boxing Day. You said you quit, right?"

"Yeah." She sighs. "Stupid hormones. I got all worked up and panicked. Marched straight into the captain's office and resigned."

"Okay, well, we need to talk about that more, but maybe it's a good thing. You need time, right? Stay here, with us, and let us love you," I say, squishing her cheeks in my hands. "I told Mum, and you know she's going to want to chat with you."

"Nic, this is your family thing. I can't just stay."

"Of course you can," Beth says, joining us. "Sorry, totally eavesdropped. Although I'm not completely sure what's going on, but Nic's right, you should be here. I never understood why you didn't come with her every year, anyway."

"Yeah, listen to Beth. She's finally said something half intelligent." I get a crust of wholemeal to the side of my face. "Please?" Tammy looks from me to Beth and suddenly bursts into tears. I'm going to go out on a limb and say this is due to those same hormones that made her up and quit her job and fake a hangover for two days.

I do the only thing I can think of and start singing *Wham* again.

# December 12th

Lining up my ingredients, I do one last sweep to make sure I have everything. I'm going to crush them all! No one builds a gingerbread house like me. We're a day late doing it, but that's fine. Tammy needed some reassurance and love yesterday. Mum spent most of the evening cuddling her. Dad gave her a pat on the shoulder and legged it out to his shed. God bless the man and his uncomfortable dad routine. Amazing how buying condoms or sanitary pads is a nonissue, but seeing a woman cry tips him over the edge. He's a conundrum.

Liam ran down to the War Room and immediately drew Tammy a picture, which made her cry harder. Liam started crying too, which led to a mass huddle in the living room trying to calm everyone the fuck down. When Niamh arrived, unaware of the situation, she looked shell-shocked. Beth managed to explain briefly before more snot and tears got in the way.

With the tea shop covered today, Mum spent the morning organising the gingerbread competition. It's the biggest one we've ever had. Usually it's just Liam, me, and Beth. This year we've added Niamh and Tammy. That's two more people I gotta beat. I'm not worried though. My building skills are unparalleled.

Beth is wearing her lucky apron, which has a decapitated gingerbread man on it. She has questionable humour. Plus, she's lost to me for the past six years. How lucky can it really be? Tammy has so far eaten two-thirds of her allotted toppings. I guess the craving thing is in full effect. Liam, as usual, ignores the rules and is already making his dough. That's cool, I'd never compete with him. Liam has no interest in beating anyone. He just wants to build something that would make Santa proud. He always adds a Polaroid photo Mum takes in with his wish list.

Niamh is the only one giving me reason to pause and possibly worry. She's organised her ingredients, and I see that glint in her eye. She has a plan. But that doesn't mean she can pull it off, right? No way she can beat the wonderland I plan to make. I'm one hundred percent sure. Okay, eighty percent sure.

"Attention gingerbread builders," Mum booms from the other end of the living room. We've had to take the competition into the lounge. The kitchen is no way near big enough for five grown adults and their individual gingerbread stations. Dad rolled his eyes when Mum evicted him from his reclining chair. I presume he's either in his workshop or has nipped down the pub for a quick pint. "The build will begin in thirty seconds. There will be no sabotage, and no shit talking."

"Mum, you said shit," Liam gasps from his table.

"Sorry kiddo, you're right. No smack talking. We keep it friendly, got it?" She shoots a pointed look Beth's way. I smirk. She sticks her tongue out at me. "In three...two...one, go!"

I'm no amateur. There's no need to panic. I've got the timings for this challenge down to a science. Tammy gathers her long ginger hair into a messy ponytail, her pale skin already flushed. She's great under pressure, so I'm not sure why this is getting under her skin. "Can first timers get any leeway?"

I snort. "No way, Sanderson, buck up and get baking."

"God, I forgot how competitive you get." She huffs.

"Ooo, Nic, I think you've got some competition over here," Mum calls. I know I shouldn't rise to it, but I can't help but look up from my station. Mum is standing beside Niamh, who is expertly mixing her dough.

My focus narrows as I watch her and I suddenly feel extremely turned on. Niamh has her long black hair tied up, wearing a Soggy Biscuit apron. Her sleeves are rolled up, leaving her forearms uncovered, and I didn't realise how much I like that. Goddamn it, I'm getting distracted.

There's a race to the oven between me and Niamh. Her little smirk when she beats me by a few seconds is infuriating and hot. Twelve minutes later, we take our cooked gingerbread templates back to our stations. Beth and Tammy are nowhere near Niamh and me now. This is a two-pony race. However, it's okay. This is where I shine. I have a steady hand for glueing the pieces together and my piping skills aren't too shabby either.

By the end of the two hours, I'm exhausted. My creation is bloody brilliant, even if I do say so myself. On my table is a winter friggin' wonderland. I'd like to see Niamh beat thi—"Jesus, fucking Christ!"

My inner gloating has come to a screeching halt. Niamh has created a full bloody Santa's village. I don't even know how it's possible. Her piping is perfect, and she decorated each house with Jelly Tots. Her gingerbread trees have scatterings of icing sugar on them, for god's sake.

"You're fucked," Beth whispers in my ear. And she isn't wrong. The only thing that will pull a win out for me is if Niamh's gingerbread is inedible.

Mum's *ho, ho, ho* notification rings out. Time is up. Amazingly, Dad appears seconds later, his attention firmly on the delicious food awaiting his judgement. I watch his eyes scan our efforts and I notice when his eyes widen at the sight of Niamh's. Game over. After twenty minutes, they declare Niamh as the queen of the gingerbread challenge. I try with all my might to look affronted, when really, I just want to get her alone to celebrate.

Tammy looks wiped, and I'm not sure if it's the baby knackering her out, or because she's finally letting herself relax. My guilt is still alive and kicking. Even if Tammy has forgiven me for my judgemental outburst, it's always going to be the thing she remembers when looking back. "Make a pot of tea, love," Mum calls. The curse of being the older child strikes again. I am and always will be the tea-making dogsbody.

The house is alive with laughter, and I guarantee ninety percent of that is Beth ripping the piss out of my losing. I can deal with it. As long as everyone is happy and enjoying themselves, that's all I care about. It's what our December tradition is all about. Speaking of traditions, I need to fill in the group about what I *didn't* find in my search of the house.

After Tammy takes herself away for a nap, I round up the troops and usher them into the War Room. "Okay, people, how are we doing?"

"Nothing at the tea shop," Niamh says. "I looked everywhere."

"Nothing in the house either," I add. "But we expected that."

"I'll do another sweep this evening," Beth comments. "We need to get over to Aileen and Wally's too."

"I want to walk Reggie," Liam interjects. My dog has been having the time of his frantic life. It's nice to have so many people around to entertain him. And, apart from the doorbell explosions, he's a lot calmer. Mostly because Dad and Liam take him out four or five times a day. I hope he remembers I'm his mum when we leave. If we leave.

"You can take Reggie out, Li. No problem. Do you want to go with Dad?"

"Yeah, he promised we could stop for a cake."

"I'm not working until tomorrow afternoon, so I can help," Niamh offers.

"Yeah, you and Niamh can go next door. Aileen will be thrilled." Beth grinning like an evil Disney witch is getting old. I need to take some revenge on my little sister. Bring her down a peg or two.

"I'm fine with that. It's been ages since I've seen either of them," Niamh answers, unaware of the raging eye-contact war.

The visit to Aileen and Wally went as expected. Aileen acted like the bloody Queen of England had popped 'round for a cuppa. I know Niamh has been around to see them since she got back from Ireland, so Aileen's behaviour was solely due to us going 'round together. In her mind, we are already a couple, I'm sure of it. Once Aileen gets something in her mind, she's a stubborn old goat.

Niamh didn't seem embarrassed by the many, *many* insinuations that she and I make a striking couple, yada, yada, yada. She just laughed it off and took another malted milk biscuit.

Now, I'm finally getting a few minutes of peace and quiet. The street is silent as the snow drifts down. The family is inside, tucked under blankets, watching the *Home Alone* movies with a ton of sugary treats. And I'm sitting on the bench in the back garden, wrapped up like a polar explorer with a mug of hot chocolate, soaking it all in. The sky is that delicious white colour you only see when it snows.

"Hey." Niamh smiles at me as she makes her way over to the bench. "Mind if I join you?"

"Of course not. I'm just enjoying the snow."

She tips her head to the sky and catches snowflakes on her tongue. A smile creeps over her face and she is so stunningly beautiful. I want to capture this exact moment and keep it close to my heart. "I can't remember the last time I sat outside in the snow."

"It's magical. One of my favourite things to do, and we've been extra lucky this year. Snow for days."

We sit in silence for a few minutes, happy to let time meander by. A small ache forms in my chest. This, right here, is all I've ever dreamed of. Not with Niamh specifically, but with someone. A person who understands my family and our bond. A woman who wants to be a part of that without getting jealous of sharing my time.

"That's a deep frown," Niamh says softly. I'm still looking at her, catching snowflakes. How she knows I'm frowning is a mystery. Her eyes haven't left the sky since she sat down.

"How?"

"It's like you project your feelings, Nic. Plus, I can see the cute forehead wrinkles in my peripherals."

"I do not have forehead wrinkles."

"Everyone has wrinkles when they frown, you eejit!"

Smoothing my fingers across my apparently wrinkled face, I sigh. "Just got a few things swimming around up here." I tap my temple a few times.

"I've been told I'm a good listener." Her nose is going pink, and she has snowflakes on her eyelashes.

"Aren't you getting cold?"

"I'm fine. So, want to talk?"

"I guess I'm worried about Tammy for a start. She hasn't told me what she's decided to do yet, but I think she wants to keep the baby."

"Yeah, that would be my guess."

"It's made me think. About how it's all going to work out."

"That's a tough thing to accomplish, considering nobody can predict the future."

She's right, of course. "I'm happy she's staying with us until after Christmas. I'm hoping it gives her some time to really digest and process."

"Ah yeah, I heard you're shacking up for the next few weeks." Niamh chuckles.

"Yeah, lucky me," I reply sarcastically. "Tammy is a pain in the arse to share a bed with."

"You could always share my bed." Um... "Did I just break your brain?"

"A little." I laugh.

"We said we could have some more fun, right? Two birds with one stone, if you stay with me for a couple of nights." She finally drops her gaze to me. "No pressure."

I smile. "I don't feel pressured. It's a very tempting offer."

"But?"

"Can you imagine Mum and Beth? Oh, let's not forget Aileen!"

Niamh rolls her eyes. "You know, the more you protest and get wound up, the more they'll do it. So what if you stay over? Let Beth make a few comments. Worth the orgasms, I'd have thought."

I swallow several times as my mind replays some of those aforementioned orgasms. They would be worth getting a bit of stick off my family. Plus, Tammy would have some space, and I wouldn't have to see a chiropractor every morning. Tammy kicks like a fucking donkey in her sleep.

I watch her breath freeze in the air. Her eyes are on me, and there's no doubt she's horny. A small and very vindictive-slash-childish part of me does an internal maniacal laugh that Pat isn't the one she wants in her bed. Well, not for now.

"Okay, I'll take you up on it. Tonight?"

"I'm not at work until the afternoon, so we can have a lay-in. I even bought extra crumpets."

I stroke my chin and narrow my eyes playfully. "It's almost like you planned to have me stay over again, Niamh O'Conner."

"Huh, weird that. So, ready to head to mine? Or we could nip to the pub for a quick pint?"

"No, Beth might want to join us."

"And you want me all alone, is that it?"

God, I love a woman who can flirt. "Something like that." I absolutely want her alone, with no possibility of getting interrupted.

I run inside and shove a fresh set of underwear in my bag. The whole family turns like meerkats when Niamh and I walk in.

"Are you off, love?" Mum asks Niamh.

"Aye, although I'm going to leave the car here if that's okay. The roads will be awful after all this snow."

"Of course. Nic, where are you going?"

I clear my throat. "I'm going to walk her home and then stay over. Tammy can have my room for the night."

Beth goes to open her mouth, but Mum grips her knee hard to keep her quiet. That's a first. "Okay, you both be careful and message when you get there."

"Will do. Night all."

We get a chorus of "Night!" before leaving.

The streets are swamped with fresh snow, enough that it's almost impossible to see where the pavement ends and the road begins. I have my trusty winter boots on, but Niamh has flimsy ankle boots that I'm positive are already soaked. "Your feet have got to be freezing," I say. She gives me a small smile and a shrug. Handing her my small bag, I step in front of her, my back to her front and squat down. "Come on, up you get."

Her laugh echoes around us. "Nic, I am not climbing on your back!"

"Come on. I'm a big, strong firefighter. I can take it. And you want to keep your feet, so giddy up."

I hear a sigh and a small grumble, but then Niamh steps forward and climbs on my back. Her legs wrap around me and her chin drops to my shoulder. If I let myself, I could believe this was the perfect moment. You know, the one where Niamh falls hopelessly in love with me. But life's not that easy. So, I'll take what I can get. And that means a night of really hot and probably very acrobatic sex.

# December 13th

A crobatic sex did not happen. By the time we got back to Niamh's cottage, she was physically shaking. Her shoes were nothing but a pair of soggy faux leather sacks. I put them in the bin the second she took them off and poured out a pint of melted snow.

My first aid training kicked in, and my libido buggered off. I was concerned she might get frostbite or hypothermia. So instead of losing clothes, I got her to put more on. I got her tucked up under a fleece blanket with a hot water bottle. We enjoyed a nice hot bowl of chicken soup and several mugs of tea. It was all very domesticated.

In bed, she snuggled into me and stayed there all night. She said she could feel the cold through to her bones and I know how awful that is. I usually run hot, but on the odd occasion I get cold, it's like I'm a frozen block of ice to the core, and the only thing that thaws me out is a boiling hot shower. Niamh didn't want to get undressed to take a bath, so I was happy to let her extract warmth from my body throughout the night.

It's now 8:45 a.m. and she's still fast asleep. To make sure she stays nice and toasty, I've spent a bit of time getting the fire up and running. Remarkable that as a firefighter, I suck at starting them. I know how, but for whatever reason, it took me forever to get the fucking thing going. Eventually I won though. Now it's belting out some decent heat. My next task is to get some breakfast on the go. Crumpets for me. Porridge and maple syrup for Niamh. She's not the only one who remembers these things. Niamh can eat a hot bowl of Ready Brek at the height of summer.

I lay everything out on a tray and make my way back to the bedroom. The blackout curtains are doing a great job of shutting out the daylight. It's going to blind the poor woman when I open them. The sun reflecting off the snow is akin to getting high-beam car lights projected into your face. I should know, it happened this morning when I opened up the living room curtains. I'm still seeing white spots.

After opening the blinds just a fraction, I sit on the bed next to the tray and do something super, super sappy. I just watch Niamh sleep. Her hair isn't beautifully spread out on the pillow; it's all over her face and partly in her mouth, which hangs open. The occasional snort joins her light snores and I can honestly say I've never seen anyone more adorable and gorgeous. Of course, I wonder if I move back up North, would she give us a chance to date properly? Exclusively too. I'd jump at the chance. I know a good thing when I see it, even if she does drool a lot.

Niamh hasn't told me anything about her ex-girlfriend, but I get the gist she was an arsehole. I can understand why she'd want some time to be by herself. But that won't be forever. Niamh told me she wants a relationship. Could that be with me if I made some changes? Am I completely bonkers for thinking any of this after a night of perfect sex, and a few days' worth of meet-ups? And what about Tammy? If I do decide to pack up and come home, could I convince her to come too? It's been on my mind. If Tammy wants to raise the baby, she'll need help. More than my inexperienced bum can offer. Mum and Dad would dote on her and the baby. It'd be like how Aileen and Wally were for me, Beth, and Liam. Tammy deserves that. Christ, I need to have a chat with her, and see if she'd be open to it.

"You're doing it again," Niamh croaks out. Jesus, she sounds terrible.

"Doing what?"

"Thinking way too feckin' loudly."

Oh, and she's a grumpy bum too. "Sorry. Hey, I brought you breakfast."

Her eye cracks open and scans the tray. Without a shred of self-consciousness, Niamh wipes the hair from her face and mouth, sniffs really loudly and then sits up. "Thanks."

"Nim, you sound terrible!"

"Well, I feel like shite, so that tracks."

"Okay, one second." I leave the room and Niamh to start her food. Grabbing my phone from the kitchen table, I overstep by calling my mum. "Morning, Mum."

"Mornin' love, everything okay?"

"Yes, and no. Niamh got really cold last night. Her shoes got drenched, and she looks like crap this morning. I really don't think she should be in the tea shop later."

"That's alright, tell her to stay put. And warm! I'll get Beth to help me out." Well, that couldn't have worked out better. Mwahahaha, suck it, Beth.

"Thanks Mum, I'll let her know. If you need another set of hands, just call okay. I can help out."

"No, no. Stay and look after Nim."

"Aye aye, Captain. See you later."

Niamh will probably be pissed because I did that, but she really should stay in the warm, so I'll take any anger and deal with it. When I get back to the bedroom, she's just finished her bowl of porridge. "Oh my god, thank you. I can't believe you remembered."

"No offence, but I watched you eat porridge in July. Not something you forget."

"Fair play. Jesus, I can't believe a bit of water in my boot has made me feel like this."

"Niamh, you had more than a bit of water. I just hope you won't develop a full cold."

"Me too. I'll swallow some cold medicine before I head to work later."

"Yeah, about that." Taking a step back from the bed, in case she decides to give me a wallop. "I called Mum and told her you wouldn't be in."

"Say again?"

Her face is difficult to read. "Um, I rang in sick on your behalf. Sorry."

She rasps out a chuckle. "You look sorry. Ah well, I'm actually relieved. Probably not very sanitary to have me like this around food."

Smiling, I step forward and sink to the bed next to her. "That's what I thought." I don't see the dead arm coming. Niamh gives me a thump. "Ow, shit."

"You should've talked to me first, Nic. I appreciate the thought, but I really don't like people deciding shite for me. I'd have happily had you do it, if you'd said something."

"Okay, okay. Sorry, I'll never do it again."

"See you don't. Well, now I have a day off. What do you want to do?"

A not-so-small part of me does a mini celebration internally. Niamh wants me to stick around for the day. Win. I haven't got any sleigh bell-related duties until tomorrow night, when I will go on my first reconnaissance mission.

"I think maybe you should go back to sleep for a little while. I'll tidy all this away and the kitchen."

"Will you come back to bed after?"

I swallow thickly. "Of course."

Liam started blowing up my phone half an hour after Niamh went back to sleep. He must have found out she wasn't feeling great because he became increasingly anxious with every message. Finally, I called him and asked if he wanted to bring Reggie over. Niamh will be happy to see Liam. He's a big teddy bear, especially when someone is feeling unwell.

Beth came with him, presumably to get out of working at the tea shop. I'll need to stop by and make sure Mum is okay. I just finish pouring water into the teapot when I hear shuffling behind me. Niamh is wrapped up in a shamrock-covered dressing gown. "It was a spoof present from my work colleagues."

"It's...lovely."

Snorting, she bimbles over. "Any chance I can snag a cup? I'm feeling a bit better." And she looks it.

"It's just got to stew for a few minutes." Niamh's kitchen has a large double window over the sink area. I pile a few dishes while keeping an eye on Reggie in the garden.

"Nic, why is there a running fluffy duster in my garden?"

Chuckling, I watch Reggie's poofy tail zoom around. "That fluffy duster would be my dog. He's carved himself a nice running track and has been out there for a good fifteen minutes nonstop." The ground is piled high with snow, and it's still falling. We can't see Reggie's body, just the top third of his tail.

"And what is Beth doing?" Niamh asks, thumbing in the direction of my sister, who is standing in the middle of Niamh's lounge, scowling.

"No idea. Shall we find out?"

"Nim!" Liam bellows, scrambling off the floor to wrap her up in a monster hug. "Are you okay?"

"I'm good, buddy. Just needed a bit of sleep. I'm happy you're here. What you watching?"

"*The Polar Express.* Want to watch it?"

"Obviously." She smiles.

I set down a tray with the teapot and three cups. Liam's quite content with a glass of milk and several bourbon biscuits.

"So, you're feeling better?" Beth asks from her standpoint in the middle of the room. Her hands are on her hips, so something is bugging her.

171

"Yeah, much. Beth, are you okay?"

"No, I'm not quite frankly!"

Whoa, okay. "Beth, what's with the attitude?"

"Nic, of all people, I don't know how you haven't said something. How can you let this stand?"

"What the bloody hell are you going on about?" Beth and her sodding dramatics.

"This," she cries, waving her hands around the room. I am utterly baffled. "Not one bauble in sight. Not even a scrap of tinsel, Nic!"

And then it clicks. Beth is throwing a fit over Niamh's Christmas-less house. "Jesus, Beth. I thought something bloody awful had happened."

"You don't think this is awful? Niamh, for shame!"

I look at Niamh, who is trying to suppress a smile. "You're fecking ridiculous, Beth Robinson."

"I'll second that!"

"She's right though, Nim," Liam comments, his eyes still trained on the television screen. "Santa won't stop if you don't decorate."

"And it's already the thirteenth of December. Your tree should have been up at least a week!" Beth adds on.

Niamh takes her time looking between us all. Clearing her throat from what I think is amusement. "In my defence,

I have been working a lot, and I live alone, so decorating seemed a bit pointless."

Beth sucks in a breath, as if Niamh just stabbed her through the fucking heart. "Pointless? To bring joy and wonder to your home. Oh no, no, no, no! This just will not do Niamh O'Conner. You're back with the Robinsons now. Christmas cheer will prevail."

Even I'm amused with Beth's antics now, and Niamh has perked up more. I smile at Beth. "So, are you suggesting a Robinson Christmas takeover?" It's not the first time. We had to do it with Aileen and Wally a few years back. Aileen wasn't well and Wally didn't have the energy to spruce their house up. Cue Mum, Dad, Beth, Liam, and me going full interior design, Chrimbo style. Their place sparkled by the end of the day, and Aileen soon felt more chipper. Mum has always said the spirit of Christmas is magic for the soul. And I tend to agree.

"I don't want to know." Niamh laughs, leaning back into the sofa, sipping her tea. "You do what you want to do."

"That sounded like a resounding yes to me," Beth exclaims. "Liam, can you sort the music?"

"On it," he replies, stopping the movie and hurrying to Niamh's sound system. Seconds later, Liam's Christmas playlist filters through the room.

"Okay, decorations. Do you have any? What about a tree?"

"Um…in the loft, I think. Everything kind of got shoved up there when I moved in."

That's my job. Being the only one who is used to heights and cramped spaces. "Ladders?"

"Spare room," Niamh answers, laughing.

Off I trot. Decorating makes me happy. Mum has usually done the majority of it by the time I arrive on the first of December. She used to wait for us all to be together to do it, but after one too many fights and squabbles, she took the option away.

The loft hatch is in the hallway just outside Niamh's bedroom. It's going to be a tiny space, considering the size of the cottage roof. Sure enough, it takes me far longer than anticipated to crawl my way around the space. I'm covered in cobwebs and dust, but I stand victorious. I found a box of decorations and a tree!

"You're not decorating looking like that," Beth proclaims, stopping me from entering the living room.

"Beth, don't be ridiculous. I'm just a bit dusty."

"Nope. Go shower. You have dead spiders in your hair. Gross!"

"I've got sweatpants you can borrow," Niamh calls from the sofa.

Banished to the shower then, I guess. Although I can't complain, fewer minutes spent with bossy Beth is probably for the best. Ten minutes later, I'm clean as a whistle. Jogging down the stairs, I fumble on the last step. Niamh has just opened the door and it only takes one glance to see Pat has turned up. Again. But this time she doesn't seem so quick to comment when she spies me over Niamh's shoulder in sweatpants, a tank top—because the cottage is boiling now—and bare feet.

"Pat, hi. I wasn't expecting you," Niamh says, unaware I'm on the stairs.

Pat narrows her eyes at me and I have to stop myself from rolling mine. "Yeah, thought we could grab lunch before you go to work." She leans in, her eyes still trained on me, and kisses Niamh on the lips.

"Oh, that's sweet, but I'm not feeling one hundred percent, so my shift has been covered."

"Not feeling well enough for work, but okay for a quick fuck, huh?"

I see Niamh rear back in surprise. "I beg your pardon."

Pat flicks her chin in my direction. I should probably make myself scarce, but she's pissed me off and I'm not leaving Niamh alone with her.

Looking over her shoulder, Niamh spots me, and for some weird reason, I wave. She rolls her eyes but is smiling. "Not so dirty now?" she says, and it had the desired effect.

Pat is going bright red.

"All clean," I reply. "You ready to get to it again?" I'm clearly referring to the decorating, but Pat doesn't know that and it makes me feel happier to get a jab in.

"I'll be right there." She turns to Pat. "I think you should leave."

"Hey now," Pat says, backtracking. "I didn't mean anything by it."

"You did, and that's enough of a red flag for me. I don't wish to see you anymore, Pat. Goodbye." And with that, Twatty Pat is no more.

Leaning against the closed door, Niamh sighs, closing her eyes. I move closer, not sure if she'd feel comfortable with me in her personal space. "Hey, you okay?"

"Yeah." She runs a hand through her hair. "She was starting to remind me of my ex. I'll never go through that again."

"Want to talk?"

She shakes her head. "Maybe later. Right now I want to see how the Robinson Christmas takeover is going."

We go back to the living room where Liam is twirling Beth around to *Rockin' Around the Christmas Tree.* The actual Christmas tree is half decorated, and it can stay like that a little longer. We've got some dancing to do. Holding out my hand, I wink. "Ready to get this party started?"

"Born ready." Niamh laughs.

# December 14th

I t's possible the Robinson Christmas takeover went a little too far. By the time we'd finished, Niamh's living room looked like Santa's workshop on acid. Beth called Mum and got her to join in later in the day. She brought four boxes full of extra decorations with her. Tammy provided us with pizza for dinner, so we ended up having quite the gathering before I threw them all out. Niamh was looking tired again, but looked like she didn't want to offend anyone by asking them to go. I have no problem doing that. Not with my family, anyway. They're not too great at reading the room sometimes.

After they all cleared out, I helped clean up, and it was kind of automatically decided I'd stay the night again. Dangerous, to say the least. Not because I wanted to jump Niamh's bones, but because it felt too comfortable with her.

We sat in the silence, watching the tree lights, and drinking tea. Far too domesticated for just a bit of fun. But I couldn't stop myself from enjoying it. It even crossed my mind to ask Niamh if we might go out on a proper date. See if there was something more between us than excellent sex. In the end, I kept my mouth shut. Niamh was still simmering over the whole Pat being a douche incident earlier, and I didn't want to come across as that arsehole who swoops in moments after someone finished with another person.

So, we went to sleep all curled up together. I woke up this morning feeling sexually frustrated and confused. Instead of sticking around and winding myself up, I made up a tiny white lie. I told Niamh that Mum called and needed me in the tea shop, knowing Niamh had the day off again.

Because I didn't want to be a liar, I headed to The Soggy Biscuit, put on an apron and spent the day serving tea, hot chocolate, and Eccles cake. By the time I got home I was kaput. Then I remembered I had my first surveillance stint. Nothing like sneaking around the neighbourhood looking for places Mum might mount a few sleigh bells in the snow to wake me up.

Beth dragged me into the War Room before I could get myself ready for this evening's shenanigans. My plan was to take a really hot bath and stay super warm until it was time to leave. Instead, I sat on the worn sofa, listening to Beth's updates. It was very funny though, when she told me she got caught snooping around Aileen and Wally's and Aileen chased her off with a broom.

It's now 9:55 p.m. and Mum is already in bed. Dad is just locking up for the night, so my plan to sneak out of the house at ten is on track. I'm dressed like a bloody goon from one of the James Bond movies. You know, the ones in all-white snowsuits with massive automatic guns. I may be sans the AK-47, but I'm packing a flask of hot chocolate.

Tammy is still not ready to talk about things. She's spending most of her time with Mum which I think is just what she needs. However, my dear best friend still finds the time to mock me mercilessly. Especially when she sees me all dressed up. She's promised not to tell Mum on me, and I sort of believe her. I think Tammy finds the whole thing amusing. She's never wanted to get involved in the search, much preferring to watch us three kids make utter tits of ourselves from the sidelines.

Beth gives me one last pep talk before I trudge outside. Mother Nature is giving me a break. The snow has stopped falling, but I still have to wade through it. Not great for stealthiness. Fingers crossed the heavens open before morning, concealing my tracks.

I have a list of places to check, courtesy of Beth and her impressive cross-referencing skills. Most of them are hard to reach, hence why I am the one doing it. We figured Mum wouldn't hide the bells somewhere too easy. There'd be too much risk that someone would come across them. We've entertained the idea that she uses speakers or something to project the sound, but we've never come across anything to substantiate the idea. Plus, when I've heard the bells, they sound too crisp, too real to be a recording.

I'm only at the bottom of our driveway and I'm already knackered. I should have worn snowshoes, or brought Reggie with me. I've seen how quickly that little guy can carve a path. He's not an option, though. He'd well and truly tired himself out yesterday.

The stars are twinkling, and the moon is bright. It's a really beautiful and peaceful evening. Jesus, what am I doing?

"What are you doing?" Niamh's voice comes out of nowhere, startling me. I can feel myself tipping over and there's bugger all I can do. My squeak of surprise is muted when my knees hit the ground and my face plunges into the freezing snow.

"Nic! Shite, are you alright?"

When Niamh finally pulls me up, I stand stunned. Sucking in a breath, I try to regulate my breathing. Thank god I put my hair up and tucked it away under my beanie. It's just my face that feels as if it's burning. "Shh-shit," I chatter. "Th-that ww-was cc-cold!"

Niamh brushes bits of snow from my face and shoulders. "Crap, I didn't mean to startle you."

"Ss-s'okay."

"Should we go back to the house, get you warmed up?"

I shake my head. I can feel my face again. "No. I'm good."

"Hmm, I'm not sure. Nic, if you get ill, I'll feel terrible."

"I won't. Maybe you could walk with me. I'll warm up soon enough."

We plod along the road in single file. Niamh traces my foot holes. It's not exactly the romantic stroll I envisioned. We finally get to my first checkpoint. It's a rather large evergreen tree. All three of us have heard the bells around this area, and there is no other place Mum could have hidden them.

"So?" Niamh looks around us. "What's happening, Nic?"

"I'm going to climb that tree," I say matter-of-factly

"Uh huh, naturally." She looks at me, amused. "Aren't you worried someone might call the police?"

I scoff. "No, it's more likely the neighbours are sitting by their windows with a bowl of popcorn waiting for me to fall on my arse."

"You're close to forty, right?" I don't have to look at her face to see the smirk.

"Few years yet, thanks. And why does my age dictate if I can climb trees?"

"Oh, far be it from me to tell you what you can do in your advanced years."

"Advanced... Cheeky sod. I'm only three years older than you. Now stop distracting me. I need to focus."

"Sorry. Please go ahead," she says while slipping her phone out of her coat pocket.

"What's that for?" Huffing, I heave my leg up to the first branch.

"Posterity." She chuckles.

Turns out, my efforts are in vain. The only thing I find up the bloody tree is an irate squirrel. The next location is a bust too. I like to believe I'm a semi-intelligent person, but Mum is stumping me. How do those bells turn up in such weird places?

"Do you think it's time for a break?" Niamh suggests. I wasn't expecting her to traipse around with me for the better part of two hours. I haven't even asked why she'd come by in the first place.

"Yeah, come on." I sigh, getting cold and irritable. We head to the park, where there is a small gazebo. Soft fairy lights hang across the beams, casting a delicate glow. We sit for a while in silence, watching our breath fog and curl in the frigid air.

"Pat showed up again."

I flick my eyes in her direction, trying to gauge her mood. She looks deflated. "At your house?"

"Yeah. She apologised again and wanted me to give her another shot."

"But it was just casual, right?" I don't know if I'm asking for me or her.

"Yeah, it was. I should have seen the warning signs earlier. She's just like my ex."

Niamh has mentioned her ex-girlfriend a couple of times but has yet to elaborate. I've never been one to push a sensitive subject, but I get the feeling she's ready to talk. I can't imagine there are a lot of people she can open up to. Her mum is lovely, however, I doubt Niamh wanted to rehash the uglier aspects of what sounds like a toxic relationship with her.

"Can I ask what happened with the ex?"

She clasps her hands on her lap as if she's physically preparing herself. "Myrna was wonderful in the beginning. I met her a week after I moved back to Ireland. We were friends in the beginning. She worked at the brewery in the admin department. Eventually she asked me out and of course I said yes. Typical lesbian situation. A few dates and we were practically living together."

"Yeah, that sounds about right. Did you get a cat?" I joke, hoping to break the tension a little.

"No, she's allergic. Anyway, things started to turn odd after a few years. We were settled, you know. Working, had a decent life. But then she started showing up when I was out with friends. Inviting herself to things, until I was never without her. I thought she just enjoyed being with me, but I can see now she was controlling. She'd bitch about people until I stopped hanging around them. Everything she said and did became passive-aggressive, and so by the time my best friend had the bollocks to say something to me, I was barely leaving the house. Only to go to work. And Myrna was there for that, too."

"Did...did she hurt you?"

Niamh shook her head. "No. It was all head games with her."

"That doesn't mean she didn't hurt you, Nim."

She leans forward so her elbows are balanced on her legs, head in hands. "Yeah, I guess you're right. There was no big blowout. I just got to the breaking point and ended it. Some of our friends knew what she was like and sympathised, but Myrna is a strong character. She never faded away from the friendship group after we broke up. I think she believed I'd come crawling back. Instead, I came home. It'd been too long since I'd focused on myself. And I'd done a lousy job visiting Mum."

"And working in the tea shop. Does that feel like a step back?" I am genuinely interested. I find myself wanting to know about her thoughts and feelings. Where she sees herself in the future.

"Not at all. It's nice. I love being a stone's throw away from Mum, even if she has a more active social life than me," she comments, laughing.

"Bloody hell, I hear you on that. At home I literally work, sleep and work some more."

"But you still enjoy being a firefighter?"

"Yeah. That's all I'll ever do but..."

"But?"

I mirror Niamh's position, leaning on my knees, cupping my head in hands. "I think it would be nice to have my family close by. You know, for the days off, and grabbing dinner together. Family stuff. My crewmates are brilliant, but they all have lives, families. Tammy has been my saving grace, but now she's quit."

"But you had a girlfriend, right? Steph."

"Yup, but that wasn't easy. None of my relationships are ever easy, and I'm tired. I moved away to get a little independence, but honestly Nim, it kinda sucks now."

"So, come home? I did, and it was the best decision."

I turn my face to her. "I've been seriously considering it." And now I'm about to be brave, or incredibly stupid. "If I did, would you be open to more than a bit of fun?"

She faces me too and her eyes look over my face. "I'd think about it."

I can't help but laugh. "Well, that's not exactly the enthusiasm I was hoping for."

She grins at me. "I didn't say no. I'm just overly cautious now. Or maybe not, if Pat is anything to go by."

"You can't shy away from people because of them, Nim. Even if you're not interested in me, someone will come along and sweep you off your feet. I hope when that happens, you keep yourself open to it."

"I never said I wasn't interested, Nic. All I want is a girlfriend who loves me and wants to settle down, maybe have a few rugrats. But on the flip side, I'm enjoying the single life. Getting to know me again."

I nod. "Completely understand that."

Sitting back up, Niamh reaches over and touches my knee. "Time is what I need, and well, if you decide Hebden is the place you want to be, don't give up. Ask me out again sometime."

"What if I've decided right now?" I grin.

She smiles and chuckles. "A little more time, Nic."

"I can do that. Now I suppose we should get back to the task at hand."

Standing, I stretch my body. That hustle up the tree is going to leave me sore in the morning. "I've got a shed to inspect."

Niamh stands up and, to my surprise, pulls me in close. "Or we could go back to mine and have some of that fun we've mentioned."

Eh, the shed can wait. Cupping the back of her neck, I draw her in. Our kiss isn't as forceful as the first time we came together. There is definitely heat, and it's going to be hot, I know that, but there seems to be something else in it now. A little understanding, maybe? Whatever it is, I'm going to run with it. I'm also going to fuck her until Pat's name is erased from her memory.

# December 15th

Jumping Jack Frost, my back is killing me! I've never had a sexual partner who likes to be fucked while I hold them up against things before. Niamh is all about that, and now my poor body is paying for it. Groaning, I roll over to search for my phone. There are a stupid amount of messages from Beth, probably wondering where I disappeared to last night. I was supposed to report back to the War Room when I'd finished scaling half the street. I did not do that, clearly.

My abdominal muscles scream at me as I roll back, bringing the small screen close to my face. It's only 6:10 a.m. and I'm wide awake. Niamh is snoring next to me in a coma-like state. Whimpering slightly as I practically fall out of bed, I rub my lower back. I need coffee. And a full body massage. Hauling gear into a burning building is less strain than a night of passion with Niamh.

She's out of crumpets, which is disappointing. I suppose I should do a shopping run if I intend to spend any more time here. And I do. After last night's talk, I'm confident Niamh will go out with me before I leave. Well before I head back, work my notice and get my house on the market.

As soon as Niamh opened that door and gave me a glimpse of a possible future with her, my decision to move back home became the easiest thing in the world. It was like this calm wave of comfort glided over my usually frustrated and conflicted mind.

I now see how unsettled I've been. And how daft. I like to think I'm a well-rounded individual with a good head on my shoulders. Sure, I'm not the most mature sometimes, especially around my siblings, but that's just family. Putting that aside, I'm a responsible adult. And yet, when it came to making a sensible decision, I couldn't do it because I immaturely couldn't handle what people might think of me coming back to Hebden. It doesn't even make sense. It's not like I had some traumatic past, or I hated living here.

It was more I thought I had to move away and forge a life separate from my family. Maybe it was my subconscious needing a break from being the eldest kid. Mum's right, I have always put a certain amount of pressure on myself to be the caretaker of the family. I guess I get it from her. Taking a closer look at myself, I guess living so far away gave me the literal space my brain needed.

I should probably talk to someone about that. That and the fact I always pick the wrong women. Tammy is spot on, and now, in my early morning reflective state, I wonder if that was another subconscious thing I did. Choosing women I could never settle down with. Meaning I left the option open to come back here without obligation.

Jesus, having fantastic sex with Niamh is marvellous for the mind. I chuckle to myself as another twinge shoots through my back. "Crap," I murmur.

"Ah, I finally broke that lovely body, huh?"

Turning on my heel, I lock eyes with Niamh, who, in all her fucking wonder, is leaning against the kitchen doorjamb wearing...a red negligee with white fluffy trim. Is she a sexy Mrs Claus?

"Not broken," I stutter, like an idiot. She's so bloody mouthwatering.

"Good answer. So, if you're not broken, I'm hoping we can..." I'm already moving toward her. My back is still reeling, but for Niamh, I'll persevere.

My fingers skim across the sheer material. "Where did this come from?" I mumble, my attention is squarely on this outfit and her cleavage. She was firmly asleep minutes ago. How is it possible she looks this good?

She shifts closer, her scent overwhelmingly delicious. "This is a gift I've wanted you to unwrap since I saw you sitting in your mum's kitchen."

"I do like presents."

"Do you not think I know how to get in your pants, Nicole Robinson?"

I grin. "You think I have a thing for Santa's wife?"

She mirrors me. "No, but I think adding a splash of Christmas magic to my accent is something you'd be into."

Her boobs are too enticing to keep up my end of the flirty banter so I plunge my face in her cleavage instead. My hands come up to cup her, running my fingers over her bra-clad nipples. Her hands gripping the back of my head hard, tells me I'm doing exactly what Niamh wants. My tongue travels from the dip in her chest up to her throat. She tastes like gingerbread, and I'm not even sure that's possible.

"Edible body powder," she gasps as I bite her neck.

Drawing my face back, I look into her eyes. Did I hear that right? "Edible body powder?"

"Mmm, gingerbread flavour."

She's perfect. I don't mean to growl, but I do, and out loud because Niamh laughs, pulling me back into her body. My tongue lashes at her skin. I can't get enough. I'm only wearing a sports bra and boxers, so it takes me no time at all to strip myself naked. Knowing Niamh's penchant for up-against-a-wall sex, I grab her backside with my hands and draw her legs up and around my waist. Oh god, she's commando. Her already wet sex rubs against my stomach. I wish I'd had the foresight of shoving my hair in a bun or something. I want her skin in my mouth, not my own locks.

"Here, let me help," she croons, gathering my hair in her hands and yanking it back. The action pulls my head, so I'm now looking up into her dark eyes. Lust is painted across her face, and it travels through me like a freight train. I feel my own excitement coat the insides of my thighs.

"I wish I was packing," I admit. I've never once worn a strap-on outside of the bedroom. It's never appealed to me until this very second. Niamh is so responsive to penetration I can get to the point of orgasm just watching her moan and writhe as I fuck her with her favourite strap.

"I want your fingers. Start with three, then add another when I'm pouring over your hand."

"Fucking Hell, Niamh." I've also never been with a woman so confident in herself and what she wants. Her body is pinned between the kitchen wall and me. Encouraging her to roll her hips, I go back to practically eating her neck.

"Fingers, Nic," she pants.

"No," I reply, because I'm about to do something that will probably realign my spine, and not in a good way. There's only so many ways you can fuck someone when holding them up. In light of my lack of strap, I want to do something to show how very appreciative I am of the effort she put in to seduce me this fine morning.

Summoning all my strength—which I must say is well above average, which is a good job considering I'm about to lift a fully grown woman up a wall—I grip under her arse cheeks, pull her body away from me slightly and lift. The squeak of surprise would be funny if I didn't need to keep full concentration. This needs to be a sexy move, not a shit-I've-just-dropped-my-lover-to-the-kitchen-floor move. Niamh recovers from her shock and throws her legs around my shoulders. My face is in direct sight of my real present. Surging forward, I pin her body hard to the wall again. One, to give my arms a rest, and two, because I want to devour her while pinching her nipples. She's securely wrapped around my head, so I get to work. My breath is a little fast due to the exertion of lifting her, but it's worth every painful and aching moment. Niamh's groans as I delve into her swollen lips are all the reward I need.

I might not be used to such athletic sex, but I excel at pleasuring a woman orally. That's not bragging, that's feedback from my many, many girlfriends. My tongue enters her, as deep as possible. It might not quite reach the spot, but it goes a long way to getting Niamh closer to the point of exploding. Her hips are canting as much as they can in such a restrictive position. I love that I'm in control. Well, I'm not really. Niamh is totally a power bottom and I'm good with that. Pleasing her seems to be my only goal in life right now. I know it should be looking for those damn bells, but Niamh has hijacked my attention wholly.

Her lips quiver beneath my tongue. Her clit is almost vibrating, or that just might be her body as I drive her nuts. My tongue is relentless as I seal my mouth around that inpatient bundle of nerves. Sucking and circling, I take confidence in her growing loudness. My fingers palm her breasts with urgency as I suck harder and longer.

It's possible she's about to break my neck with the vice grip of her thighs, but what a way to go. My face is buried so deep, I can't breathe either. Sex with Niamh is a threat to life, but god, I want her again and again. As the thought races across my mind, a scream I have never heard from her echoes around the kitchen. Only when she pulls my head back by my hair, do I stop.

"You're going to kill me," she gasps, looking down. Her head is almost touching the ceiling. Full of adrenaline, I'm still able to hold her up with my shoulders and hands.

"You are amazing."

She swipes two fingers across my chin. "That was amazing." Giving one last cheeky swipe across her slit, I grab her arse again and manoeuvre her back to solid ground.

"Shite, I can't stand." She giggles. "My legs are like jelly." A bit like my arms, I'm guessing. As much as I would like an orgasm, I want to lie down and nap.

"Nicole Adelaide Robinson. Where have you been?"

I stop in the doorway to my parents' living room. Tammy is sitting in the single recliner with Reggie on her lap like she's a bloody Bond villain. "My middle name is *not* Adelaide."

"It doesn't matter. You didn't come home last night. I was up worrying!"

Slipping off my coat, I sink into the sofa. "Sorry, Tam, I thought you'd be passed out."

"I was, but then I woke up expecting to spoon you, and guess what? No big spoon to speak of."

I roll my eyes. "Tammy, you don't spoon, you koala for half an hour and then kick me in the kidneys."

"But that's how we sleep together."

"Well, I was sleeping with Niamh last night."

She grins. "I'm glad you were the one to bring up Ms Nim. Now you can't get pissy when I ask questions."

"Want to bet."

"But I'm pregnant and vulnerable," she pouts.

I laugh out loud. "Christ, so that's it. You'll play the preggo card anytime you want something?"

Shrugging, she smiles. "Might as well."

I'm about to test the waters. I want to give Tammy as much time as she needs, but I need to factor her into my future plans, which means we have to talk. "So, does that mean you've processed?"

She spends a few moments stroking Reggie's head. He's draped over her with his tongue lolling out the side of his mouth. His front paw twitching now and then. "Yeah, I think so. Your mum has really helped."

"Can I ask what you've decided?"

Nodding, she lets out a small puff of air. "I'm going to keep the baby. I think I knew that from the start, but I freaked out. It's why I up and quit in a moment of panic. Deep down I knew I'd be a mum to this little one," she says, patting her abdomen. "I can't be a firefighter and a single mum. Well, I could, but I don't want to put myself in dangerous situations with my baby waiting at home for me."

Moving from my seat, I walk over, lean down and kiss her on the forehead. Squatting to look in her eyes, I take her hands. "You're going to be a wonderful mum, Tam. And I'm here for you, every step of the way."

I see a tear form and drop down her cheek. She must be feeling so overwhelmed. "It's all quite scary," she sobs.

Reggie startles before rounding on Tammy and licking her face. The little guy is an emotional sponge. Tammy's laughing within a few seconds, and my dog is satisfied that he has done his duty. Enough that he hops onto the sofa and promptly falls back to sleep on his back with all four legs in the air.

"I-I haven't worked out how I'm going to live just yet," she gasps. "I'll need a job, but something flexible."

Clearing my throat, I tug on her hand to catch her attention. "I've been thinking about it," I begin. "H-how would you feel about moving in with me, up here?" Tammy is rarely lost for words, but I've successfully rendered her mute. "Before you give me a list of reasons why you couldn't possibly ask all that of me, hear me out, okay?" She nods, so I carry on. "After this whole bag of crap with Stephanie, I'm ready to change things up. I've been ready for a while, really. As much as I love my house and the guys at the station, I want to come home. It's just taken a few conversations to finally get that through my dense head. You're my best friend, Tam, and I want to be there for you and the little one. Mum and Dad would fall over themselves to be grandparents, and you know they see you as another Robinson. We could move up here, get a small house together, and start fresh. You'll have support, and I'll have my family."

"Are you being serious?" She still hasn't moved a muscle.

"Completely. I spoke to Dad about wanting to move here, and the reasons I've been struggling with that."

"Which are?"

"Unimportant now, Tam. The fact is, it all just makes sense, doesn't it? We'd be a family."

"And when you meet someone? You aren't going to want me and a kiddie hanging around."

"I'll have the same rules as I do with the family December tradition. It comes with the territory. Any woman that can't deal with that or with you won't make it past the front step."

"But—"

"Will you just think about it, please?"

Thankfully, she nods and smiles. "Of course, Nic. I'm just shocked."

"Let's give it till the end of Christmas."

She pulls me into a fierce hug. "I love you, Nic."

"Love you too, Tam."

"Now, let's talk about Niamh?"

# December 16th

I t felt really good spending yesterday afternoon and evening with Tammy. Even though she grilled me relentlessly about Niamh. Only when Mum came home with Liam did she shut up. It felt a bit like old times, though. Laughing and joking together. Beth gave me a hard time for a while, but eventually, even she chilled out.

I have to admit it took more self-control than I thought to not message Niamh. We'd already spent several nights together, and I knew if I didn't take a break, I'd be setting myself up. Niamh needs time, and I intend to give that to her, but it's really fucking hard to take it slow when I'm around her. We're supposed to be just having fun, but my treacherous heart is already pining for more.

I woke up feeling less sore than I predicted. At least I don't have to go to the gym. Mum was up at the crack of dawn to open the tea shop. We had a cup of tea together before she bustled off. Normally I'd be worried she was overdoing it, but I can see that she loves what she does and she has help. Once again, it's something I need to work on. I'd love someone to tell me when I became this neurotic person. Was it before or after Liam's accident? Speaking of the man, he's just stormed through the front door like a tornado. That's not good. There's not much that could upset him in his favourite time of the year.

Standing in the kitchen doorway, I wait for my dad to come in. I know they took Reggie for a walk. It's become a morning ritual for them and Reg loves it. On cue, my energetic pooch comes skidding through the door and launches himself into a wiggle dance when he sees me. It's nice to know he still recognises me as his mum. With all the love and attention he gets here, I couldn't blame him for shifting his allegiance to the people that give him bacon bits on the sly.

Dad follows shortly after, looking upset and confused. He always scratches his forehead when something perplexes him.

"What's up with Li?" I ask the moment he closes the front door. Reggie is doing laps of the living room.

"I really don't know, love. We had a lovely walk. Built a snowdog, fed the ducks. We stopped by Niamh's on the way home, and you know how Liam gets. He doesn't want to be babied all the time, so I let him knock on Niamh's door alone while I took Reg a little further down the street. Well, next thing I know, Liam comes storming down the path, his eyes full of tears and doesn't say a blasted thing. I had to jog to keep up with him."

Setting the tea towel on the kitchen worktop, I head upstairs, patting Dad on the shoulder as I go past. "I'll see if I can figure it out," I say.

Beth is still asleep, but I'll wake her if I can't get through to Liam. She's great at cheering him up. Failing that, I'll call on Tammy.

Knocking on his door produces nothing at all, so I gently open it and pop my head through the crack. I can see Liam's hulking mass under his duvet. I can also hear him sniffling. Shit, a crying Liam breaks my fucking heart. What the hell could have happened?

"Liam?" My voice is low and calm. I don't want him to hear my worry. Still nothing. Walking over to his window, I draw his blackout curtains closed, press play on his stereo system and switch on his fairy lights. Liam has a mini version of the decorations in the living room. It's his very own Santa's grotto, and it calms him. With carols playing softly in the background, I sit on his bed and pull the duvet from over his head.

Liam immediately hides his head behind his huge hands, which makes me smile. I notice he's changed into his Christmas Grinch jumper. That means he doesn't want to talk. Another coping mechanism Mum and Dad came up with to help him. He has several jumpers and t-shirts that represent his need for space. The Grinch is an apt choice for this time of the year. I think I've only ever seen him wear it once.

"Buddy, will you talk to me?" He shakes his head and momentarily removes his hand from his face to point to the grumpy Grinch on his chest. "I know, but I really need to know what has made you so upset, mate."

It takes him several minutes before he finally opens up. "I-I went to see Nim. I wanted to remind her about the Christmas market. She said we could go and eat all the chocolate. But Nim didn't answer the door, that woman did."

It takes a second for my brain to connect the dots and my heart doesn't like the answer at all.

"Do you mean Pat?"

He nods and hiccups. "I asked why she was there because she wasn't Nim's girlfriend. And she said she was, and that Nim was tired of me always coming around. She-she said Nim just doesn't know how to tell me to go away."

Fisting my hands, I take a beat to calm down. "You didn't see Nim at all?"

He shakes his head. "No, but the horrible woman said Nim didn't want to go anywhere with me, and the only reason she is my friend is…is because she feels sorry for me that I have no friends."

Framing Liam's face with my hands, I look him straight in the eye. "Liam, I promise on Santa himself what she said is not true."

"On Santa?"

"Yeah, that's how serious I am. Nim is your best friend, and that other woman is just stupid. Please don't believe her."

Liam sits up and draws his legs to his chest. "She's like Jack Frost," he stammers. I know he's referring to Jack Frost in *Santa Claus 3*.

"Yeah, she is. Now, why don't you take a few minutes to calm down? Let's put Mr Grinch away and I'll get Dad to put on a DVD. Reggie would love you to snuggle him on the sofa."

"O-okay."

"Good man. See you downstairs." I leave him and my rage finally rises to the surface. Liam is untouchable as far as I am concerned. You can take the piss out of me, even my sister and parents, because they know how to defend themselves, but antagonising Liam. Oh no. Who the fuck does Pat think she is? I'll have to look past the fact that Niamh obviously invited her over in the first place. That's a separate issue, I can't deal with right now.

Taking the stairs two at a time, I skid to a stop at the front door. Pulling on my boots and winter jacket, I let my anger simmer. I'm not a violent person, and I won't lay a finger on Pat. She's not worth the trouble that would bring. She does, however, need an education on what is tolerated in this town.

After calling out a strained, "I'll be back soon." I head outside.

Dad and Liam have created a nice walking path through the snow that takes me all the way to Niamh's cottage. A place that up to this morning held sizzling memories. Now I feel nothing but white-hot anger.

I knock on the door in my usual manner. It takes a second before the door opens and a startled Niamh stares back at me in her short robe. Guess I can tell why she invited Pat over then. Her eyes are wide, and she goes to speak, but I cut her off.

"Is Pat still here?" My voice is calm.

"Um...y-yeah, in the kitchen." I see her swallow hard.

"Mind if I have a quick word with her?"

Niamh's eyebrows crease. "Sure."

Smiling, I slip past her and head to the kitchen. Pat is sitting at the table in a pair of boxers and a t-shirt, her hair messy. A smirk forms on her face when she sees me walking through the hall towards her. She leans back casually, and I want to laugh. She's a fucking clown.

The grin soon fades as I walk right up to her, tipping the chair she is on backwards until it's only on two legs. Her arms flail about, but I'm not going to drop her. I just want her off balance. Bringing my face close enough she can feel my breath, I speak quietly.

208

"If you ever speak to my brother like that again, Pat, I will bury you. And no, that is not a threat, it's a promise. In fact, don't utter a fucking word to any member of my family again. Understood?"

"I...was just joking," she stammers out.

"Understood?" I repeat. She nods. Letting the chair bump back to the floor, I stand slowly, never breaking eye contact. When I'm convinced that she's got the point, I turn to face Niamh, who is standing by the worktop, looking utterly confused. She takes a step towards me as I go to leave. Her hand latches on to my forearm. We stand silent for a second. My gaze wanders down to her hand, and she retracts it.

"Our fun is over." Her breath hitches, which is weird. Looking up from my arm to her eyes, I see unshed tears. "I *do* know when to walk away from a red flag." And then I leave.

Beth and Tammy are in the kitchen sipping coffee when I return. My anger has transformed into disappointment. How could Niamh want to be anywhere near someone like Pat. She's the poster child for what makes a toxic relationship.

If it weren't so early in the morning still, I'd be necking eggnog until I couldn't stand. At least Liam seems to be okay now. Reggie is sprawled across his chest, snoring as Liam strokes his belly. I'm going to talk to Mum and Dad about getting him a dog of his own.

"Hey, where have you been?" Beth asks. "And why do you look like you want to murder someone?"

My hair is windswept, and I probably look insane. "If you see Pat, you do not speak to her. If you see Pat with Niamh, you don't speak to either of them. Is that clear?" I don't mean to sound so aggressive, but I think my frustration is finally about to explode.

"Whoa, what's happened?"

"Is that clear, Beth?" I growl.

"Stop getting pissy at me," she bites back. "I've not done a thing to warrant this, Nic."

Gritting my teeth, I storm upstairs, change into my gym wear and head to the basement. It's probably been a good six or seven years since I used Liam's punch bag, but I'm about to unleash hell on that thing. I detest feeling this angry. It's not who I am. I'm a chill person who wants to help people, not punch their lights out. But the anger I feel towards Pat is overwhelming.

Sweat drips from every inch of my body. God knows how long I've been at it, but my arms are sore, and my breathing laboured. It's done the trick, though. I feel so much better for pounding the crap out of the bag. I've also come to the conclusion that if I weren't so sex blind over Niamh, I wouldn't have reacted so strongly to Pat.

We've dealt with people in the past being ignorant and downright cruel where Liam is concerned, and I've never flipped out like that before. It's because my stupid heart attached itself to Niamh and a fantasy I thought might one day become reality. I'm usually so wary of women, because I know how it will end. I don't give myself freely anymore, but then Niamh walked into my parents' kitchen two weeks ago and took something from me. My ability to keep a distance. The bubble wrap I'd so securely placed around my heart is being popped one little bubble at a time. But now it's time to re-secure the wrapping. Especially if I'm going to be seeing her more often.

I'm still punching the crap out of the bag when the music I've been listening to is cut off. Dropping my arms, I turn, expecting either Beth, Tammy, or Mum. I'm not expecting Niamh. She's standing there fiddling with her top sleeves. Her hair is up in a ponytail, and her clothes look comfy. "Hi."

Slipping off my sparring gloves, I take the towel draped over the back of the old couch and wipe my face so I can see properly. "What's up."

"Can we talk?" I don't like to hear her sounding so small.

"Sure."

I gesture for her to sit on the sofa. I'm a disgusting mess, so remain standing. Niamh rubs her forehead, her eyes cast to the floor. "I'm sorry, Nic."

Taking a large mouthful of water, I let her words wash over me. "You didn't speak to Liam like shit, nothing to apologise for."

"You know I don't mean just that."

I shrug. "Still nothing to apologise for. You can sleep with whomever you like. We were only a bit of fun. I know that."

My heart cracks with every syllable. I don't have a right to be angry with her. She was super clear where her head was at and I willingly went along with it. If anyone is to blame, it's me.

Niamh finally looks up and into my eyes. "I...I'm still sorry."

Dropping the towel and my water, I cross my arms. It's a protective stance, I know that. "I think it's best if our fun comes to an end."

"I ended it with Pat."

"Well, okay. Still, not my business."

"Please don't be like that, Nic."

I shake my head. "Niamh, I'm not sure what you want from me. But I know I don't want to play games. I've had more than enough of that over the years. Pat's an arsehole, but I think you know that. However, it's entirely up to you if you want to sleep with her. I don't have a say in that."

"But what if I want you to?" Niamh stands and walks a little closer. "I want to spend time with you, Nic."

"Niamh, you have literally just left another woman, who I'm guessing you had sex with. A woman you told me reminded you of your abusive ex. Forgive me if I don't believe that you really know what you want."

"I...it was a mistake."

"And that's for you to figure out. Look, I think it's best if you stick to chilling with Liam, and we take some distance."

"I don't want distance," she growls. I'm so bloody confused. "I want you to stay with me and do all the things we were planning."

By all the things, she means the Christmas market, ice skating, and movie marathon. Things we'd talked about after sex, when we were curled around each other. You know, things that a couple might do. Things I'd fooled myself into thinking were possible.

"And once we've done those things, will you be giving Pat a call?" That was bitchy.

"No. I shouldn't have done that. Not least because you're right, and she is the worst, but because I knew it would upset you if you found out."

"We made no promises," I reply.

"No, but I asked you to wait."

"You did. And I would have."

"Past tense?"

Jesus, I want to kiss her. How insane is that? "I don't know."

# December 17th

The days are passing way too fast and with far too much drama. Thankfully, Niamh didn't push our conversation in the War Room any farther, instead she spent the rest of the day with Liam. I heard through the Robinson grapevine she promised Liam he would never have to deal with Pat again. That's good enough for me. I trust Niamh wouldn't make him a promise she couldn't keep. As for me, I spent the day with Tammy. I also spent a lot of time grovelling to Beth. This year has been rather turbulent as sisters. We usually wind each other up, but it's rare we argue or genuinely upset each other. That's on me, and I told her so.

I've called a family meeting for this afternoon. Mum finishes at the shop in an hour, and Dad promised to stop fiddling in his workshop long enough for me to sit them all down and talk seriously about my life decisions. I've been home seventeen days, and that might not seem like a lot, but it's long enough to know I'm ready to stop being stubborn and start planning my homecoming. I've made a list of things that need my immediate attention. Talking to my station manager being the first.

"Spencer," he says in his gruff voice. I get on well with Graham Spencer. He's a nice, down-to-earth guy. Treats the crew fairly, but pushes us to be our best.

"Boss, it's Robinson."

"Ah, Robinson, how are you? How's the family?" Another thing I really like about him is his understanding. He's met Liam and the rest of the family. He knows why I save my yearly allotted holiday time for December, and never once questioned it.

"Ha, bonkers as usual. Mum says she'll send me back with a batch of mince pies."

"She's a damn fine woman. My waistline won't thank her, but the rest of me will."

Graham has a low-key crush on my mum, which is *ick*. The way to that man's heart really is through his stomach, and the moment he tried my mum's sweet delights—that sounds wrong now, I hear it—he was a bit besotted. My dad laughs it off, smiling proudly that he gets to love my mum. It's super sweet and explains why they've been happily married for so long.

"She's alright." I laugh. "Liam says hi, and so do Beth and Dad."

"Cracked the case yet?"

"I'm not sure it's possible. Those bloody bells will still be taunting me until I'm an old woman."

"I have faith in you, Robinson. Now, to what do I owe the pleasure of this call?"

"Right...so, um."

"Wow, I don't think I've ever heard you stutter so much. It must be bad!"

"Not bad, just... Ugh, I'd like to request a transfer to the Hebden station." There, done, plaster ripped off.

Graham releases a rush of air. "I can't say I'm overly surprised. Finally made the decision, huh?"

I have no idea how he knows I was even considering it. "Um, yeah?"

He barks a deep laugh down the phone. "Robinson, I know everything that goes on in my station. Don't worry, I won't say anything to the crew. You're sure this is what you want?"

I take a second to look out my bedroom window. The street looks so beautiful, coated in a thick layer of snow. "Yeah. It's what I want."

"Then consider it done. You'll need to come back after Christmas to start the process. I'll ring Paddy and let him know he's getting a fine firefighter."

"Thanks, Graham. It's been awesome serving with you."

"Of course it has. I'm brilliant. We'll organise a sendoff with everyone when we have a firm moving date."

"Copy that, sir. See you in a couple of weeks."

Well, that went easier than expected. I never thought Station Manager Spencer would have an issue with it. It's just the end of an era. Plus, he's losing Tammy as well. I wonder if he guessed her decision somewhat swayed my own.

I'm nervous about the family meeting, and I don't know why. Mum and Dad have already told me they'd be happy If I moved back. Liam's going to hit the roof. But what about Beth? Will she think I'm a loser for coming back? After all, she's a successful vet, with a great guy, living in Scotland. She's made something of herself.

Where is all this self-doubt and flagellation coming from?

"Are you making sandwiches?" Beth asks as she hops on the kitchen worktop.

"I am. Thought it would be nice to have some food while we all talk."

She eyes me suspiciously. "Okay. Are you going to tell me why we're having a family meeting? You aren't pregnant too, are you?"

I roll my eyes and then bat her hand away as she swipes a sandwich, shoving the whole thing in her mouth. I have to stop myself from bursting with laughter the second she realises it was a cheese and Marmite one. The half-masticated sandwich hits the kitchen floor with a dull thud. Beth starts scraping her tongue, gagging.

Mum walks in earlier than expected and observes Beth. "Marmite?" she says. I nod. "Need a hand, love?"

"No, I got it. Why don't you try to get Dad to down tools early?"

"On it." Dad is terrible at sticking to plans when he's tinkering in his shed. Liam is already in the living room watching television. Setting the food on the coffee table, I sit on the footstool in front of the sofa. That way, I can see everyone. Dad grumbles as Mum ushers him into the living room. Beth tucks herself in the corner of the couch, still trying to wipe any remnants of Marmite from her mouth.

"Thank you for agreeing to this," I begin. "It won't take too long. Um, after a lot of thought, I've made the decision to come back up North. For good."

Liam throws the remote control out of excitement and rugby tackles me from the stool. We land in a heap on the floor. "You're coming back, for good?" he asks into my neck.

I laugh and wheeze at the same time. "Buddy, you need to let me up. I can't breathe."

"Sorry, Nic Nic." He scrambles to his knees and hauls me up.

"Yeah, that's what I mean, Li. I'm going to move closer to you. Is that okay?"

He's already nodding before I've finished my sentence. "Yes. I can't wait, Nic Nic." He leans closer to me and whispers, far too loudly, "We can look for the bells and Santa all the time." I laugh and kiss his cheek. "Maybe. But Santa takes a break in the year, so I'm not sure we would get lucky."

"Hmmm. Yeah, that's true. Well, we can play football and take Reggie out."

"That's a good plan, mate."

"I'm going to tell him." I presume he wants to inform my dog we are moving. Reggie is outside, rolling in snow. "Don't worry, Mum, I will put on my boots, coat, and scarf."

"Good lad," she replies, smiling. We all watch him leave before resuming the conversation.

"So, what do the rest of you think?" My eyes stray to Beth, who is looking strained. Oh god, she *does* think I'm a loser.

"You know how we feel, sweetie," Mum says, her hand resting on my dad's. "I can't wait to have you closer. We can help look for a house to rent or buy. Have you any preference?"

"Only that it will need to be a three bedroom. I've asked Tammy to move with me. She'll need help, and I want her to have a family around her."

Mum leans forward and cups my face. "That's awfully nice of you, Nic."

"She's family, right?" I say to everyone.

"She sure is. Oh, I get to be a grandma!"

We titter at Mum's enthusiasm. Dad is beaming, so I'll take that as a yes. He's pleased with the news. Beth still hasn't spoken. "Beth? What do you think?"

"I think you suck, Nic!"

"Bethany," Dad chastises.

Beth rolls her eyes. "I was going to tell everyone that Ted and I are engaged and have secured premises here in Hebden to open a new veterinary clinic!"

Mum's squeal brings Liam rushing back in, looking terrified. "What's wrong?"

Beth is engulfed by a blubbering Linda Robinson. Her words are totally incoherent. Dad is laughing but has tears in his eyes. I'm smiling from ear to ear, which helps Liam come down a few notches. "Mum," Beth grumbles.

"Oh, all my babies are coming home!"

"Now that's a wonderful Christmas present," Dad remarks.

"I can't believe you didn't tell me," I say over the sobbing. Beth finally bats Mum away and stands up. "War Room, let's give this pair a few minutes to relax." She laughs. Mum is curled up in Dad's chest crying.

"Come on, Liam. Grab Reggie and meet us downstairs."

"Okay, Nic."

Beth is throwing darts at the board when I arrive in the War Room. "Engaged. I can't believe you were able to keep it a secret for so long," I say, picking up the spare darts and readying myself to take my turn.

"Well, I wanted to tell you when Ted arrives, but I thought it wasn't worth it after your announcement. Why didn't you tell me you wanted to come back?"

I throw my first dart. I suck at this game. "I dunno, Beth. Suppose I didn't want you to think less of me."

"You are so dumb."

"Thanks. Now, where did your decision come from? I thought you liked living in Scotland?"

"We do, but I've always said that if we thought about having kids, I'd want to be close to Mum. Ted's family is nice, but we're not that close to them. And Ted loves you lot."

"He's a cool dude."

"So, we're both moving back. Jesus, is the town big enough?" She chuckles.

"I'm sure we'll be okay. Does this mean you are thinking of kids?"

"Not right now, but after the wedding. You're my maid of honour by the way, and Liam is my best man."

"Isn't Ted supposed to have a best man?"

"He will. He'll also have a maid of honour. Screw tradition."

Liam's thundering steps catch our attention. He's holding Reggie like a rugby ball. "Are you both really coming home?" There are tears in his eyes. Bloody hell, we'll need a year's supply of Kleenex at this rate.

Beth and I nod, then brace ourselves for the inevitable tackle.

It took Mum all afternoon to calm down. She was still sniffling through her meat and potato pie. After dinner, Beth went to call Ted, and Liam decided he needed to watch all the Santa Claus movies in his room. As for me, I enjoyed a peaceful evening swiping through the local real estate ads. Tammy was suspiciously absent all day, and only came back around nine. She wasn't forthcoming in explaining her absence, which is fair. She's an adult. But something made me suspicious. Call it best friend intuition.

I'm actually looking forward to an early night. I've put a row of cushions down the centre of the bed in an attempt to create a kidney kicking buffer.

Tammy laughs when she sees my creation. "You think cushions will keep you safe." She cackles. "My dear Nicole. Such a fool."

We're ribbing each other when Liam barges into my room. "Nic, we have a problem," he says. Instead of being dressed in his PJs, Liam is clothed in ski trousers, coat, and scarf.

"What's wrong?" I climb out of bed and immediately get dressed.

"Beth is stuck," he hisses. Mum and Dad are still downstairs watching television. How did they not notice Liam?

"Stuck? What do you mean?"

"She's stuck up on a roof!"

Tammy snorts, which isn't helpful. "I've gotta see this," she adds, getting herself dressed again.

"How the bloody hell is she stuck on a roof? She's supposed to be in her bedroom."

"I know," Liam states. "But then she said she wanted to do a check of the street. Said it'd been too long since we'd looked for the bells, and she went outside. I went too, because I didn't want her to be alone, but then she saw something on the roof across the street. The little roof, you know the bungalow, and then she climbs the wooden thing attached to the wall. And then she was stuck."

His rushed explanation is a little hard to compute, but I get the gist. There's a reason I do the climbing in this family. Every bugger else is scared of heights. "Do Mum and Dad know?"

He shakes his head quickly. "No, we sneaked out. Beth's really good at it."

Oh, I know she is. She always snuck out when we were kids, leaving me to panic about her safety. Tammy steps to my side with a grin and her phone. "This is going to be great."

"This is going to get us arrested," I murmur.

"Can you save her, Nic?" Liam asks, and he looks on the verge of a panic attack.

"I'll go get her. Liam, I need you to stay here, okay? If Mum checks on you and you're gone, she's going to freak out. Can you do that?"

"Yeah, can I keep Reggie in my room?"

"Sure thing. And I'll come and see you when I get back, okay? There's no need to worry."

"Okay. Be careful, Nic."

Tammy and I ninja walk down the stairs. My parents are too busy howling at something on the box. We manage to get our coats and boots on without getting caught. The street is deadly silent when we step outside. Looking around, there is no one I can see. Most houses on the street have their curtains drawn. That'll help. Maybe we won't end up in the local police station.

Crunching down the garden and across the street, I stop in the road when I see a silhouette clinging to the chimney of Mr Patel's bungalow. I was hoping that Liam was exaggerating, but no. Beth is, in fact, stuck on a roof, and I have to get her down. Wonderful.

# December 18th

Thank god Mr Patel is as deaf as a doorknob. There's no way we could get away with Beth pretending to be a large pigeon or anything. She must be causing all sorts of weird noises as she clings to the bloody chimney top like a chuffing Gekko. It's been over three hours since Liam told me she was stuck on a roof, and I'm yet to find a way to get her down. Not because I'm incapable, but because Beth literally *will not* let go of the chimney stack.

"Beth, you have to trust me," I hiss. I'm on the roof now too. It took me all of two minutes to climb up, and in any other circumstances I would make my way over and forcibly remove her, but the snow is tricky and I can't be certain there isn't ice. Mum would murder us if we fell off a roof right before Christmas.

"I don't want to die," she wails dramatically.

"Will you keep it down!"

"Oh, I'm sorry," she growls. "Forgive me for expressing my very valid concerns."

"They are not valid because you won't die, for fuck's sakes. If you let go and take my hand, I can get us safely to the ground and you can have a drink in the warm." I need to be in the warm. My feet are blocks of ice and I forgot to put on gloves.

"You can't promise we won't fall and get mangled on Mr Patel's pointy bushes."

"I can promise you will die of hypothermia if you don't move your arse. We've been out here for hours?"

"Stop being dramatic!"

"Bethany, do not talk to me about dramatic right now. And yes, it has been hours. It's past midnight, we're into a new day for crying out loud. You could have been tucked up in bed ages ago. So stop being stubborn and let me get you down. Because Bethany Grace Robinson, if you don't, I'm going to have no choice but to call the fire brigade. Which means this entire street will be lit up like a Christmas tree with red and blue lights. And you know what that means? Mum. We'll have to deal with an irate Linda Robinson, and I don't know about you, but I could really do without that!"

I think I've finally got through to her because I see her white-knuckle death grip finally loosen. She slides slowly down to her knees so she's straddling the peak of the roof. "What do I need to do?" she asks, her voice wobbly with fear.

"That's good. Start sliding towards me. Keep in the middle and use the top tiles to help you move. Nice and smooth."

I'm glad Tammy got bored ages ago and went back inside. As amusing as it is, I know my sister has a real fear of heights, and being mocked is the last thing she needs. That can wait until the morning, and I know there is video footage.

It takes a long time for Beth to slide her way to me. I'm really not sure how she made it up here in the first place. The trellis she used is at the other end of where she ended up. "Okay, Beth, now I need you to swing your leg over slowly so you're facing me." I'm at the edge of the roof on my knees.

"But I'll slip down," she sobs.

"No, you won't, I promise." She tentatively brings her knee over the apex of the roof. She's still on her bum, but now she's facing me. Leaning forward, I lay on my stomach and reach to take her leg. "Inch towards me. I've got you."

She swallows thickly, but does as I ask. Her arse is going to be frozen by the time I get her down. Beth grasps me tightly when she's in reach and I sit there holding her for a few minutes. "I can't climb down the trellis, Nic."

I'm in agreement. She's been up here too long, and her legs are stiff. Hell, my legs are stiff. Pulling out my phone, I call Tammy. Nothing. She's more than likely snoring. I can't call Liam. I could try... "Shit," I grit out. Beth is starting to shake. There is a ladder by the garage. "Listen, I need to get down and grab that ladder." Why didn't I do that in the first place?

"No, don't leave me, Nic."

"Okay, calm down. Just give me a second." Stabbing the contact icon, I hold my breath. I'm not sure if I want Niamh to pick up. What if Pat picks up? No, she promised Liam, Pat was history.

"Nic?"

Her voice is scratchy with sleep. "I'm so sorry for waking you up," I begin, "but I have an emergency."

"Is Liam okay?"

"He's fine. It's his dipshit sister that needs help."

"Which dipshit sister." She chuckles.

"Rude." I laugh. "Beth, she's, um...stuck on a roof, and I need a ladder."

"Sorry, can you repeat that?"

"You heard correctly. Beth's on Mr Patel's roof, and she won't let me get down to fetch the ladder. It's like twenty feet away, but she's gripping me like we're hanging off the side of a bloody cliff." Beth pokes me in my ribs, but her grip intensifies. "Tammy isn't picking up and I can't call Mum."

"God no, she'll go ape. Okay, I'll be there in a few minutes."

"Thank you."

"Is she coming to help?"

"Yes, but it's really unnecessary, Beth. I could be down there in a second."

"No, just hold on to me, please, Nic."

I huff but don't move. I've gotten her this far. I don't want her to start panicking again. "What possessed you to do this, Beth?"

"I wanted some fresh air, so I snuck out. I only planned to go up and down the street a few times. You know, stretch my legs. I love the street when it's all snowy. Anyway, I looked up and saw something shining in the moonlight and I got so excited. I really thought we'd finally found something. I went on autopilot, and the next thing I know I'm by Mr Patel's chimney."

"I take it the shiny thing wasn't bell-related?"

"No, it was an old aerial bracket. That's when I realised where I was and how high up. I just froze."

"Liam was supposed to be in bed."

"Oh, stop being Miss Responsible for like a second, Nic. We were just walking around the street. He's not a kid."

"I know that," I reply hotly. "But Mum would skin us alive if anything happened to him again."

"But nothing would happen. He's still a grown man, even with his difficulties."

"Has he said something?"

She sighs. "He just wishes he could do more things with us."

"I don't want him to feel left out."

"He doesn't, but he also understands that we treat him a little differently than we do each other. He gets sad that me and you can nip down to the pub, but he has to stay at home."

I'd never thought of it that way. "He could come to the pub."

"Yeah, he could if we offered. Mum wouldn't like it, but Liam doesn't want to drink. He just wants to be included in some more adult stuff, you know."

"God, I feel awful."

"Nicole, I didn't tell you, so you could add another brick of guilt to your chest. Jesus, you gotta stop seeing us as your wards. You might be the eldest, but that doesn't mean you are responsible for us. How many times do I need to say it?"

"Jesus, you're feisty."

"I'm cold," she grumbles. "But it's still true, Nic. I'm really excited you're moving back. But please leave the worrying and crap for Mum and Dad. That's their job, not yours. Oh, and also we need to speak about whatever the hell is going on with Niamh."

"Speaking of," I say when I see a shadow slip silently down the side of the bungalow. "We'll talk later, okay," I whisper. Beth nods.

"Can the Robinson kids go one night without causing mayhem," Niamh calls up quietly. I really love her accent.

234

"Only one Robinson caused this," I reply. "The ladder is just over there." I point. Beth and I sit silently as Niamh wades through the snow and retrieves the ladder.

There's a small clatter as she lines it up close to where we are waiting. "Just stand on the bottom rung, Niamh. Keep it steady." She nods. "Okay, Beth, ready to go home?"

"Yeah."

"Nice and slow. Keep hold of my hand and use your foot to find the top rung." Her body is shaky, but she finds the ladder and slowly begins her descent. Niamh is at the bottom, ready to catch her. They hug and Beth sobs quietly. I quickly descend and move the ladder back. Beth's legs give out.

"Nic, she's not going to be able to walk," Niamh whispers. Not thinking twice, I scoop her up in my arms.

We make our way to the house quickly and quietly. Niamh holds the door open and checks that my parents are not around. I'd have been surprised, but you never know. I take the stairs two at a time and get Beth tucked up in bed. She has an abundance of blankets I pile up so she's extra warm. "Thanks, Nic," she whispers before closing her eyes.

Niamh is still by the front door when I creep down. I know my next words are probably a mistake, but I don't seem to be able to think clearly when she's around. "Do you want to stay?"

I don't know what it is about her that makes me do silly things like invite her to stay with me. In my bed. I promised myself I would take a step back. Niamh's decision to sleep with Pat is still at the forefront of my mind, and although she promised Liam Pat was gone, I'm still feeling a little hurt, if I'm totally honest.

Over the past eighteen days, I'd thought we'd become close. Well, closer than mere fuck buddies. Sure, there'd been a lot of sex, but also things in between, like movies, and dinners, and breakfasts. After finding Pat sitting at her kitchen table the other day, I felt foolish. But a part of me couldn't believe I'd made our closeness up in my head.

Maybe that's why I invited Niamh to stay. To talk and hash things out, once and for all. If, by the end of the conversation, Niamh was only interested in sex, I'd walk away. I know she asked me to wait for her, and ask her out on a proper date, which I said I would, but after the Pat incident, I'm not going to put my heart on the line for someone who won't take care of it. Seventeen girlfriends later tells me I've done that way too many times already.

The house is silent, save for a few creaks here and there. Niamh is lying next to me, wide awake. I'm desperately trying not to start babbling out of nerves.

"I'm sorry," she whispers.

Turning to look at her, I decide it's time to put my big girl knickers on and act like a bloody adult.

"Want to tell me what happened? I mean, I know you said you wanted time, but you also said you knew Pat was toxic. I have to say it hurt seeing her sitting at your table. Especially just a few hours after we'd been together."

She swallows several times before turning away from the ceiling. "You scare me, Nicole." Well, I wasn't expecting that. "I kind of swore off the idea of getting with someone again after Myrna. That's why Pat seemed like a good choice in the beginning. And why I wanted no strings with you. Sex without the complications. But then I should have known better." She laughs quietly. "I'd always had a soft spot for you, Nicole Robinson. I just didn't expect to start feeling things so quickly, and when I realised I was getting in deeper and deeper, I sabotaged myself by going back to Pat."

"You could have just talked to me, Niamh. We're not twenty-something's anymore who need to play games. We're also friends, I thought. I don't want you to feel uncomfortable around me. If you needed to stop sleeping with me, you could have just been honest."

Her hand snakes into mine under the covers. "That's the thing, Nic. Not sleeping with you is the absolute opposite of what I want. That's the scary thing. I want to see if we could do this, you know, be a couple. Go on dates."

It's my turn to swallow several times. "We can do that." I yawn.

"Where is Tammy?"

"In with Beth. She woke up when we got home and thought it would be a good idea for Beth to have someone stay with her."

"Can we talk more tomorrow?" Niamh asks through a mirrored yawn. I nod and instinctively pull her into my arms, where we fall asleep.

I slept like the dead, and so did everyone else. It's a rare thing for the family to all have a lay-in, but that's what happened. Most of December is planned out. Mum goes to a lot of trouble to set up Christmas-related activities for us to do. Partly for Liam, but mainly because we all love it. However, there are days where we simply relax in our PJs watching television all day. Even Dad doesn't leave the house to tinker in his shed. Today is one of those days, and Niamh has been there for it all. No one mentioned the fact she'd magically appeared from upstairs, or that Beth was a little quieter than usual. Mum has been glowing all day, still high on the news that her two girls are moving close to home.

The late-night conversation is yet to be picked up again, but I'm not too worried. It's given me time to mull over what Niamh had to say. I understand why her feelings for me could be unnerving. I've never had a partner who treated me the way Myrna treated her. I've had a couple that were less than stable, but in the end, I came out unscathed, for the most part.

The fact Niamh has had a soft spot for me makes me feel all fuzzy. And, the fact that she's here, quite happily participating in my family's festive traditions, sets rockets off in my chest. She's in my spare onesie again. We've watched numerous Christmas films and eaten junk. There's been sibling squabbling, and inside jokes, but Niamh has had a smile on her face the entire time.

A hand on my shoulder jerks me out of my reverie. Beth leans in, her voice low. "The countdown is on, Nic. The bells will sound tomorrow."

# December 19th

I still have Beth's Dickensian warning rattling around my head. "Tomorrow the bells will sound," I imitate, chuckling to myself. She just needed a set of chains hanging around her neck to really sell it.

However, she wasn't wrong. In all the drama I'd forgotten that on the nineteenth, one of us would hear the sleigh bells for the first time. It happens every year without fail. So, our day off yesterday was probably a good thing, because none of us Robinson kids will be relaxing now. I had really hoped we would have found something prior to today, but once again, our plans have been thwarted. We're on the defensive as usual.

Beth is on point today. By the time Tammy and I ambled downstairs to grab a coffee and toast, Beth was already up and dressed, waiting for us. She barked orders to grab breakfast and meet her in the War Room. Tammy rolled her eyes and stayed put in the kitchen. I did as I was told.

Liam is draped over the couch when I arrive. "Morning, Li," I call.

"Hey, Nic."

"So," I say, standing in front of Beth. "What's the plan, General?"

"Glad you asked." Tapping a pen to her chin. "I think we need to think outside the box today. And by that, I mean not leave the house."

Scrunching up my face, I try to get her angle. "Sorry, how is that thinking outside the box? It's not like we haven't done that in the past."

"Not to the extreme I'm suggesting. I'm talking about refusing to leave the kitchen all day until the clock strikes midnight."

"You want us to bunk down in the kitchen?"

"Yep. Think about it, Nic. Mum can't set up the bells with us in there. I'm sure she's already devised a way to get one of us out of the house. It'll be something like seeing Aileen or Wally."

"Or buying milk," Liam adds.

"Exactly." Beth smiles, pointing at our little brother who is immensely satisfied with his contribution. "It's the same every year, and we don't realise what's happening until it's done."

"So, by doing nothing, we might just scupper the bells. Do we want to do that?"

"Yeah, won't Santa be upset?" Liam asks.

"No, I don't think so, Li. There will be four other days for Santa to shake his bells." I grimace at Beth and she reflects it when she replays her words. "And we only want to prove a theory."

"Do we?" I ask because my brain is a bit on the slow side this morning.

Beth huffs dramatically, which makes Liam giggle. I smile at him and wink. "Yes, Nic. We want to prove that Mum is setting up the bells beforehand...for Santa."

"But we know that," I argue.

"Do we? We've never proven it. Once we can say for definite, it means the bells are out there somewhere just waiting. Like Niamh said, we need to change our M.O. Once the bells start ringing, our carefully laid out searches go up the spout."

"I don't want to stay in all day tomorrow, Beth. It's the Christmas market, and I'm going with Nim," Liam says excitedly.

"Don't worry, buddy, we're all going to the market. That's why I chose to do it today."

"Okay." Liam is happy with that. I was hoping to head over to see Niamh and have that chat. It's like we're in this weird limbo. I'm not sure if she wants me to ask her out now or not.

"Nic?"

"Yeah, fine. I can hole up in the kitchen for a day." I'll message Niamh and let her know, even though she's none the wiser about my plans. I just want to stay in contact.

"Mum's not going to be happy," Liam says. "She's baking mince pies for the market, and you know she gets scary if we get in her way."

"On second thought though," I begin, my mind puzzling through every conceivable outcome of my mother's squirrelly ways. "We know she can't be doing this alone. So even if we're in the kitchen watching over her, there's nothing stopping one of her minions from setting up the bells."

Beth nods her head in contemplation. "You're right, and you know how much it pains me to admit that, sis." I roll my eyes. "Okay, new plan. We're going to take Mum, Dad, Aileen, and Wally hostage."

"Wow, that escalated quickly." I laugh.

"Eh, they've seen us do worse. Nic, you go and get Aileen and Wally. Make sure you confiscate their mobiles."

"There's a hundred percent chance Wally has no idea he even has a mobile."

"Good point. Just Aileen's then. Tell them they're coming over for lunch. Liam, can you get Dad in the living room?"

"Yeah, I can do it, Beth. Should I take his phone too?"

"No, I'll get that. Dad always leaves it on the shelf near the back door," Beth remarks.

"So that leaves you with Mum," I say, making a mental note of what we're all supposed to be doing and the likelihood it will go tits up relatively quickly.

"Yes, I'll take care of Mum. Once all phones have been collected, we'll lock the house up and wait it out."

"Well, it's certainly a break from the norm." I chuckle. "Do you think we've finally lost the plot?"

"Nim will come over after work," Liam calls. "I just messaged her and asked for a scone."

My heart does a little happy dance. "Good thinking, mate. The whole team should be here."

"So, we all agree?"

I shrug my shoulders. "If we're going to prison, might as well be together. Come on, let's go kidnap the family."

At the top of the War Room stairs, we split off and go our separate ways. Getting Aileen and Wally over here shouldn't be too difficult. Aileen will want a good gossip session with Mum and I'll offer Dad's single malt whiskey to Wally. That's a done deal right there.

As predicted, my job was easy. I settle Wally in the recliner with a full tumbler. Dad is looking a little confused, which is understandable. Liam, in all his massive glory, is refusing to let him out of the living room. Mum's raised voice alerts me to Beth's task at hand, and I'm almost afraid to go and see if everything is still on track.

I do my best not to crack up, but it's hard. There is a standoff in the kitchen. Mum with her apron on, hands across her chest glaring at an equally rigid Beth whose hands are on hips. "Nicole, tell your sister she's being ridiculous, and to hand my phone back."

Shaking my head, I sit at the kitchen table. "Sorry, Mum. No can do. It's only until midnight."

"Only until... Oh, for heaven's sake! This is about the bells, isn't it?"

"Tell us how you do it, and we go back to our lives," Beth says, her eyes lasered on Mum.

Throwing her hands up, Mum laughs. "I've told you every year, it's magic."

"Fine," Beth huffs. "House arrest it is, then."

Mum looks from me to Beth. "You're serious." She laughs.

I nod. "Yup. And we have your little helpers." Screwing her eyebrows up, Mum pushes past Beth and goes to the living room. Beth takes the opportunity to lock the back door and slip the key in her pocket. "I'll get the front door."

I stick my head in the living room to check on the inmates. Mum is sitting next to Aileen, and they're both shaking their heads laughing. Wally slowly sips his nip of whiskey, and Dad still looks confused, but is working on his own whiskey tumbler. It's going to be an interesting day.

"If you insist on getting in my way, you could at least help," Mum grumbles. To be fair, Beth is taking her job of babysitting Mum seriously. Maybe too seriously. There's no way Mum can call any bell helpers, so Beth doesn't need to be stuck to her side.

"You know I can't bake," Beth replies, trying to snag a cooling mince pie off the tray. She gets her arse whooped with Mum's Santa tea towel.

Mum shakes her head. "I can't wait for Ted to arrive. You might find something better to do then."

"Oh, I forgot to mention. Ted's bringing his sister. Is that okay?"

"Sure, the more the merrier." Mum loves a full house on Christmas. She went through a phase of trying to wrangle the neighbours into joining us for Christmas dinner, which we always have on Christmas Eve. Dad finally got her to stop when we literally couldn't fit another body in the house.

"Where's Tammy?" It's suddenly occurred to me that once again my bestie is absent. "She's never here."

Mum leans against the worktop, sipping on what looks like a chocolate Irish coffee. "At the tea shop, love. She's taken quite a shine to it, and I think the work is helping her cope, you know."

Tammy has never been very good at just stopping. She's one of those people that has to keep moving. "Has she spoken about the prospect of moving here?" I'm being nosy and should wait for Tammy to come to me.

"She has, but I'm not discussing that with you, Nicole. Just like I wouldn't divulge our private conversations."

"Ha, told ya." Beth grins.

"Fine. So, what's new with you, Mum?"

She rolls her eyes. "Are you really going to barricade us in this house all day? Haven't you got better things to do?"

"Nope," Beth and I say in chorus.

"Nim is on her way," Liam bellows from the living room. "She's going to do the secret knock, and then the handshake, so we know it's her."

Beth looks over at me. "We have a secret handshake?"

"*We* don't." I laugh. "Liam and Nim do."

"Huh. I want one. Come on, let's make one up." And just like that, we are two gangly pre-teens making up silly handshakes. Better than dance routines, I suppose, although we made a killer Ace of Base routine one year.

We've made a pretty elaborate handshake that I'm ninety percent sure we will forget in about ten minutes. A loud *rat-a-tat-tat* on the front door interrupts our practice time. Liam flies to greet—Nim, I presume—with so much excitement Reggie starts howling. Wally starts laughing hysterically at my dog's behaviour. I think he's well on the way to being tipsy. Wally, not Reggie.

Beth hauls me from my seat, and towards the new guests-slash-prisoners. It's guests plural because Tammy is with Niamh. "Why does Liam want to search us?" Tammy asks, causing me to laugh.

"Sorry, it's the rules. We need your phones, too."

"Nicole, you are not taking my phone!"

"But Tam Tam, you gotta give it up to come in. It's the rules, and you always tell me I should play by the rules." Aha, god love my brother. Tammy can't refuse him anything.

Scowling at me for some reason, she hands over her phone and allows Liam to do a pat down. Now, because he's a gentleman, he doesn't get in all her nooks and crannies.

Thankfully, I don't have that issue. Once Liam moves on to Niamh, I step in front of Tammy with a grin. "Spread 'em."

"You're ridiculous. Although it's been a few weeks since I had any action, so I might enjoy it," she replies deadpan. Chuckling, I give her a once-over.

"She's clean," I call. "Mum's baking, and there are spares." Tammy's eyes light up and she scuttles away.

Niamh steps up to me. "Should I spread 'em too?"

Beth mock gags. "Ugh, come on, Liam. Let's go."

"Are you feeling sick, Beth?" he asks.

"Yeah, will you watch the telly with me for a bit?"

"Of course. Cuddle Reggie, he's really good at making me feel better. I bet it would work for you, too."

Niamh and I watch Liam and Beth walk away, chatting. The surrounding air suddenly feels a lot heavier. I'm far too aware of how close Niamh is to me and the fact my entire family is just a room away. "I need to…"

"Feel away," she almost purrs. I am seconds away from hitching her over my shoulder and taking her upstairs to do wicked and exhilarating things to her when my mum bursts the bubble.

"Dinner is in fifteen minutes." That's everyone's cue to get off their backsides and get things ready. Mum likes to set up the dining room table as if the queen was coming to tea any time she had a full house to feed.

Biting my lip, I give Niamh a thorough once-over, and yes, I can't help but squeeze her hips just a little. I want to convey how much she affects me. "Can I stay tonight?" she asks and I nod.

I lean in and give her a soft kiss. "I'd like that."

Once again, it feels like something has shifted or maybe evolved. I now know where her head is at. We have a chance to build something new, and we're both a little scared.

Mum delivers a signature Toad in the Hole with mashed potatoes, green beans, and gravy. Everyone is tucking in, me included, but I guarantee no one is thinking what I'm thinking. Well, maybe Niamh is. The conversation is relaxed, and I take a second from my dirty thoughts to look around the table. All my favourite people are here. This right here is why I have never given in to pressure from partners to give up our Christmas tradition. Our impromptu kidnapping has turned into a family dinner party.

The candles on the table add to the homely atmosphere. It's already dark outside, and the snow has started falling again. There's a gentle murmur as we all start slipping into a food coma. That is, until Beth, Liam, and I go stiff, our heads shoot up and look at each other. It's impossible. Mum and Dad are still talking, not paying the blindest bit of attention. Aileen is poking Wally, who has definitely fallen asleep, and Tammy is stabbing her leftover peas paying none of us any attention. Niamh is looking at me, confused.

"Did you hear that?" Liam gasps.

"It can't be," I mumble, looking around the room. "You heard it right," I ask Beth.

"Yes, but how?"

"I heard them too," Niamh says, wide-eyed. As far as I'm aware, it's only ever been us Robinson kids who have heard the sleigh bells. Without missing another second, we push away from the table and start searching. Mum squeals when Liam practically picks her up to look under her chair. Wally snorts awake and starts laughing again. Tammy rolls her eyes but doesn't move and Aileen and Dad carry on eating their pudding.

We search for a good half an hour before the four of us collapse into the War Room. Niamh still looks shell-shocked. "I... I can't believe I heard them," she gasps. Her eyes crinkle with a smile.

"Told you the bells would toll," Beth huffs.

"Yeah, but that begs the question of how?" Maybe Mum is on to something with this magic malarky.

# December 20th

Mum left early this morning to open up the tea shop. Early enough that she avoided a three-kid interrogation. Dad slipped out with Reggie, too.

We ended up having a sleepover in the War Room. None of us could come up with a plausible reason for how we'd all heard the bloody bells while sitting in the dining room. Especially not after keeping everyone in the house and away from technology. Liam firmly believes that Mum is an elf. And honestly, I'm inclined to agree.

We put our confusion and suspicion on the back burner because today is Christmas Market Day. I think it's the day we all enjoy the most. Mum has her own stall with the thousands of mince pies she's baked. Plus, a huge vat of her famous hot chocolate. Dad has a small spot on her table where he sells mini wood carvings. They're always Christmas-based. He's quite skilled. I've tried to get him to sell them full-time, but he always tells me it would take the joy out of making them, which is fair.

The streets are packed with all sorts of vendors. I think it's the one day that gets me feeling giddy, just like I was when I was small. There is so much Christmas magic in the air, it's impossible not to love it. Plus, this year Niamh is coming along. I'm not sure in what capacity yet, but I intend to find out. Is she coming as Liam's bestie? A friend of the family? Or as my plus one. I'm not going to label it as a date, because I don't want to jinx anything.

"Hey, Nic, can you walk with me for a bit?" Tammy asks quietly. We've only just stepped out of the house, and my feet are already cold. Niamh gives me a smile and catches up to Liam. We begin our trek through the snow towards the village.

"Everything okay?"

Tammy links arms with me and rests her head on my shoulder. "I'm going to do it. Move up here with you."

I stop us and pull her in for a hug. "Ah, you've made my day, Tam."

Smiling, she squeezes me back. "But with one caveat."

"Okay."

"I'm not moving in with you." I go to protest, but she holds up a hand to stop me. "I love you for offering, but I'd like to live by myself. I'm going to be a single mum, and that's okay. I know I'll have you and the rest of the family to help. I won't be alone in that regard."

"Never. You'll have all the help you want."

"I know, which is why it's not so scary thinking about the future anymore. I'm going to work at the tea shop and live in the flat above. Your mum and I have it all figured out, and I'm happy. So, you have to be happy and not give me any shit."

"Wow, okay." I laugh. "No shit-giving here, I promise. I'm just happy you're going to be close still."

"Me too. Have you thought about where you want to live?"

"I've glanced at some websites. I might rent for a little while. Did I tell you I rang the boss?" The solid punch to my arms tells me I forgot to let her know.

"No, you didn't, you arse. Was he okay? Is he mad? Does he hate me?"

"Shut your trap and I'll tell you." That earns me a second punch and a dead arm. "He's putting in a call to the station in Hebden. I'm waiting to hear from the station manager there. And Spencer wasn't pissed."

She nods and we start walking again. "It's falling into place pretty well, huh?"

"Yeah, almost like I'm actually doing the right thing." I grin.

"You are. Now, what about Niamh?"

Taking a few cleansing breaths, I study the very woman Tammy wants to talk about. She's laughing at something Liam is saying. "She's really great, Tam. But you know, after the whole Pat thing, I'm a little nervous."

"Didn't she talk to you about that?"

I look at my best friend quizzically. "How did you know?"

"Who the bloody hell do you think convinced her to open up, you pleb?"

We stop walking again. If things continue like this, we won't reach the market. "What do you mean? Did you speak to her about me?"

"Well, yeah. For once you picked a good one and I couldn't sit by while the pair of you fucked it up before ever really giving it a chance."

"Tammy!"

"I know, I know. I crossed some boundaries. So sue me. Did you guys talk it out or what?"

"Yeah. I mean, she still needs a bit of time, but now I know she's not in it just for sex. I'm okay to wait."

"I don't think you'll be waiting long, Nic. She's had her eye on you from day one. Even longer if I'm to read into what she's told me."

"She said she had a crush on me when we were younger."

"Figures. So, is there a plan or are ya just gonna wait for her to make the next move?"

I blow out a puff of air. "I mean we've already slept together."

"Yeah, but now you need to do some wooing."

"I want to ask her on a date, but what if she shoots me down?"

"It's possible. Given she hasn't told you how much time she needs. But after last night, I think you're safe."

"Will you two hurry up," Mum calls.

"We'll meet you there!" I scream back. Niamh's gaze rests on me for a little longer before she takes Liam's arm again. "What did you see last night?"

"More a feeling, Nic. She couldn't stop looking at you, and clearly feels really comfortable. I get she doesn't want to rush it. Myrna was a cunt."

"Tammy!"

"Well, she was. Anyway, I know it's made her reticent to jump into something, but she knows you. If I were a betting woman, I'd say you could ask her on a date to say, ice-skating, and she'd be happy to go."

"Did she say that?"

"Christ, Nicole. This isn't high school. I'm not going to write her a note for you. You're nearly forty. Ask her out!"

"Blimey, you're crabby. Alright, I'll see how it goes at the market and then ask, okay?"

"Good. Okay, next item on the agenda. What are you buying me for Christmas?"

"Ted's stuck in traffic. He's going to be late," Beth grumbles.

"That just means you get to stay longer at the market," Mum says. We've been helping her out for the past ten minutes. People in Hebden really like her hot chocolate.

"Yeah, but I wanted to have a stroll around it with him," Beth whines. I wish I'd have gone with Dad and Liam now to the Merry Go Round. The owner of the rides dresses all the horses in tinsel and Santa hats. You'd think it was Liam who loved it, but it's actually Dad.

"Mind if I sneak off for a bit?" I ask Mum quietly. She sees my eyes roaming over Niamh, who is just across the way, looking at homemade Christmas ornaments. Her sly grin and wink, plus the little shove, tells me I'm good to go.

"Hi, see anything you like?" That came out a little saucier than expected. The raised eyebrow and small smirk hits me like a brick. How can a few facial movements render me so incapable of doing...anything?

"There might be something I'm thinking of picking up," she coos, her accent thicker. I know she does it for effect, and why wouldn't she? It works!

"You know what I mean," I reply, laughing. "Fancy taking a walk around with me?"

She places a delicate bauble with an intricate glass snowflake trapped inside back on its cushion. I'll swing back and buy that for her later. "I'd love to. What about some hot cider and a stuffed Yorkshire pudding?"

"Sounds heavenly. You know, the crew I work with couldn't get their heads around a Yorkshire pudding wrap."

"Why, it's just like a fajita, but English."

"Bloody Southerners." I laugh.

Everything with Niamh is easy. There is a heaviness between us, but it's not uncomfortable. Well, maybe a little in the crotch area. Walking along, we come across the Hebden Bridge LGBTQIA+ stall, and of course they have the calendars on sale. They must have hauled ass to get them printed in time. I'm hoping Niamh doesn't notice, but of course she does and makes a beeline toward it.

Caroline Markson, a lovely woman and dedicated volunteer, is manning the stall. Her smile is wide and bright as we approach. She looks half frozen, but then I see several discarded hot cider cups beside her. There's a definite warm glow about her cheeks. "Oh look, it's two of our calendar girls." She giggles. Yeah, she's absolutely tipsy.

"Caroline," Niamh says, leaning in to give her a one-armed hug. "How are the sales looking?"

"Tip top. I think we're well on our way to selling more than last year."

Niamh turns to me with a twinkle in her eye. "I can understand why they are going like hotcakes. The December model alone is reason enough."

I blush like an idiot, because any attention from her makes me hot under the collar.

"Are you two?" Caroline wiggles her fingers at the two of us. I look at Niamh because she's the one that started flirting.

"I'll take two calendars," Niamh says, bypassing Caroline's question. I'm not sure how to take it.

Swallowing my disappointment, I plaster on a smile. "Two?"

"Sure, one for the tea shop, and one for my place."

We fall silent as Caroline bags up the calendars. A quick "goodbye" and we're off. Our stroll is slow and now and then we bump shoulders. Considering I have fucked this woman up against several surfaces, we're acting far too shy with each other.

I'm just about to say something when I feel her hand slip into mine. In front of other people! That means something, right? Nibbling my lip, I decide to take a leap of faith. "Would you like to go ice skating with me tomorrow?"

"That would be fun." She smiles.

"Just to be clear, I'm asking you on a date." No way I'm leaving room for miscommunication.

"Well, I kinda figured, Nic." She chuckles. "I'd love to."

"Cool, great, yeah, awesome." Jesus. Niamh raises her eyebrows at me, and I roll my eyes. "Please ignore that."

"It's cute when you get all flustered."

My joy and embarrassment are temporarily forgotten as I spot Pat in the distance. She's got her eyes firmly on Niamh and our linked hands. I'm gearing myself up for a confrontation when I see her shoulders slump and she walks in the opposite direction.

We continue to browse the stalls. The hot cider and Yorkshire pudding wrap really ended the day on a high. I want to invite her back with me, but I think that might be pushing it. I'd rather prepare a kickass date for tomorrow. It feels like the beginning of us, and even though we've had sex, I want to wait until after our date to do it again. Don't get me wrong, doing naughty things with Niamh is at the top of my list of things I want to repeat. However, those experiences were lust-fuelled. I'd like to see if our chemistry is the same after we've spent time getting to know each other on a deeper level.

"I'm visiting Mum tonight, otherwise I'd invite you over," she says.

"Will you say hello from me?"

"Of course. Maybe you could come with me one day?"

"Sure, I'd love to."

An irritated-looking Beth thankfully interrupts our awkwardness. "I heard the fuckers again!" she proclaims, causing several people to look our way. "I was by the canal, watching the ducks, and I heard them."

"That's a new location," I say. "We need to add that to the map."

"How is she doing it?" Beth asks, throwing her hands in the air in frustration. "Hang on... You're holding hands. In public."

Niamh gives me a little squeeze. "Trying it on for size." She grins.

"Liam is going to lose his mind." Dread plummets my heart to my stomach. "Nic, chill out. I don't mean in a bad way. He's wanted you two to get together for ages."

"He has?" I can feel some of the colour returning to my face.

"I already spoke to him," Niamh interjects.

I look at her, dumbstruck. "You have?"

"Bloody hell, Nic. You're not doing much to endear yourself right now." Beth scoffs playfully.

"I'm very endeared," Niamh answers. I'm speechless. Here's me worrying about asking her out on a date, and she's already spoken to Liam about us being together. And she's endeared by me. "It's her arms, Beth. You should see what she can—"

"Ew, no. Nim, what the hell! Ugh, you suck. Okay, I'm heading home to wait for Ted."

Niamh is laughing beside me. We watch Beth wind her way through the crowd. She's a force of nature, that woman. "You really spoke to Liam?"

She pulls me to the edge of the market, where several stone benches stand unoccupied. We sit, our hands still clasped. "Is that okay?"

"Um, yeah, I just wasn't expecting it."

She nods her head in understanding. "I spoke to him on the way here, actually. I-I've been chatting with Tammy. And, well, I really don't want to bugger up my chances with you because of the past. I like you, Nic. A lot, and it's not because you can bench press a car and lift me up walls, although that definitely works in your favour. I mean, wow, talk about hot."

Pinching her thigh playfully, I laugh along. "Okay, stop that. I can do, *in the moment*, dirty talk, but I'm just going to blush if you talk about it now."

She leans in and kisses me oh-so-softly. This isn't rushed, or lust-filled. Her tongue gently caresses my bottom lip, and I let her in. The kiss is slow and deep. My hand begins to wander up her thigh. I want her, but not like this. I want to lay her in a warm bed and take my time. I want to explore each other's bodies all night long and learn all the ways that make her feel good. We pull away at the same time and spend a few moments looking at each other.

"I really like you too, Niamh."

Niamh smiles. Her face is a little flushed. "Shall we head back? Beth will want to debrief in the War Room."

If I were a hopeless romantic, I think this moment would be *the* moment where I look back and realise I fell in love with Niamh O'Conner.

# December 21st

I've never met Ted's sister, Morgan, before today. Morgan had already left for her hotel by the time I got home last night. Instead of the debrief I expected, Beth was far too wrapped up in Ted to talk about the bells, which was fine by me. My grey matter was still firmly on Niamh.

I'll remember this day for one reason. It's a solid reason to etch the memory into my brain bank because it's not very often I sit down to eat breakfast in a half-sleep coma, only to be confronted with a live animal on the table.

Two beady black eyes staring at you is more than enough reason to scream like a child, in my opinion.

Now the aforementioned animal was in a cage, and if I had not still had one foot in the Land of Nod, I would have noticed when entering the kitchen. My toast ended up somewhere near the backdoor, and my tea got launched up the wall. Reggie was in food scrap heaven, and Beth was her usual self and laughed her arse off.

"What in the hell is that?" I manage to choke out.

"It's a beaver," Liam announces, as if it's the most regular thing in the world to have one in the kitchen.

My head is on a swivel as I take in the furry critter, Liam's smile, Beth's tear-stained face due to her excessive mockery of me, and Ted's warm smile.

"Why is there a beaver in the house?" And why am I the only one who is surprised by this? "Does Mum know?"

"Of course she does," Ted answers kindly. "Morgan couldn't take Betsy to the hotel, so your mum agreed to let her bunk here."

"Betsy?"

"Yeah." Ted grins. "Nic, meet Betsy Beaverton Munch."

My mouth opens and closes like my pet goldfish I had when I was eight. "Sorry, can you repeat that?"

Ted chuckles. "Betsy Beaverton Munch."

"That's one hell of a name."

Beth has collected herself enough to talk. "Morgan named her. Betsy was brought into the clinic when she was just a pup. We're not sure what happened to her mother. Anyway, Morgan took her on, and now they're like best buds."

"But...she's a wild animal!"

"Not anymore. Betsy couldn't survive in the wild." Ted comments as he bends down to look Betsy in the face.

"So... Morgan just has a pet beaver." I can't tell you how hard it is not to make inappropriate jokes.

Ted chuckles. "She sure does. She reckons that if she can't get a human beaver to stick around, she might as well embrace Betsy." Beth is back to cackling again when she sees my face. Ted's shoulders are shaking with laughter, too. "My sister has a sense of humour."

"So, Morgan's gay?"

"Queer. That's how she labels herself. And she's never been one to follow social norms, so for her, a pet beaver is totally acceptable."

"But Betsy Beaverton Munch. That's a little on the nose." I laugh.

The back door opens and in strides a woman with aqua blue hair, black-rimmed glasses and facial piercings.

"It is on the nose, isn't it?" She laughs. "Hi, I'm Morgan. You must be the famous Nicole. Beth adores you."

I stand and fling my arm around Beth, who is fire engine red. "Ah, I adore her too."

Beth playfully bats me away. "Enough of that. How's the hotel, Morgan?"

"Lovely. I miss Betsy though. But she seems happy enough." A knock on the front door interrupts the conversation. As usual, Liam rushes to answer it, nearly knocking us over like bowling pins. I hear voices and am delighted to see Niamh walking down the hall. Her eyes never leave Liam as he chatters on about Betsy. My eyes never leave her body because no matter what she wears, Niamh is stunning.

Stopping in the doorway, Niamh surveys the rather crowded kitchen. "Morning everyone."

"Look, here's Betsy," Liam says, dragging Niamh over the threshold. "I told you she's a beaver."

"You sure did Li. Um...can I ask?" Waving her hand in the direction of Betsy. Who, I might add, is very chill in the presence of so many gawking humans.

I'm about to open my mouth to answer when Morgan slides in, her eyes roaming all over Niamh. I want to be mad at her obvious ogling, but that would be hypercritical.

"Betsy is my pet beaver. Hi, I'm Morgan."

"Oh, Ted's sister. Nice to meet you. I'm Niamh."

Morgan extends her hand in greeting. She then proceeds to lift Niamh's knuckles to her lips. Are we in the eighteen hundreds? Who kisses hands anymore? "Enchantée." I see Ted roll his eyes, and Beth laugh. Niamh grins, which kinda hurts, because the thought of her enjoying the attention of another woman dents my ego. "Would you like to get a drink later?"

Jesus, Morgan doesn't muck about, does she? It's taken me over twenty days to pluck up the courage and ask Niamh on a date, which is supposed to happen today. Maybe she'd prefer to hang out with the enigmatic Morgan. I wouldn't blame her. Morgan is cute as hell, and all mysterious. And she has a pet beaver for crying out loud. I don't have a beaver. Well, I do... Oh, you know what I mean!

"As tempting as that offer is, I'm going to have to decline."

"I'm a really good date." Morgan smiles, her hand still holding Niamh's.

"Alas," Niamh sighs dramatically, "My heart beats for another."

"She's one lucky lady."

Niamh casts her eyes to me, and I'm sure I look like a stunned cartoon character. "I don't know. I think we're both lucky."

Morgan's head turns to me. "Well damn, Nicole. Way to go."

"Um...thanks?" This is such a weird situation. Beth snorts, which I think deserves a dead arm. Before we can devolve into our former youthful selves and embarrass the hell out of each other by squabbling and giving Chinese burns, Ted intervenes.

"Why don't we all go to the tea shop and grab brunch? We can talk about the wedding plans." That is why I love Ted. He knows exactly how to distract my sister.

"Good plan, bro. I just need to walk Betsy around the garden."

"Okay, you walk your beaver and we'll get ourselves ready," Beth says straight-faced. I cannot be the only one holding back the very obvious cracks about Morgan and her beaver, right? Ah, nope, I'm not. Niamh has a twinkle in her eye, and I can see she's clamping down on her lip, probably to stop herself from laughing.

Needing to be a little closer, I sidle up to Niamh and speak quietly. "Want to go ice skating after?"

She turns slightly with a warm smile that I know is just for me. "Love too. I can't promise I'll stay on my feet a lot."

"I'll catch you." It seems I've suddenly entered a Hallmark movie.

"Cheesy."

"Yeah, I heard it." I laugh.

Mum is practically bouncing off the ceiling when we all filter into the tea shop. Her eyes light up with such happiness it steals my breath a little. I suppose I never really thought of how much Mum would miss us when we moved away. The thing I love most about her is that she never lost herself when she became a parent. Same goes for Dad. They kept their lives as partners. As much as they doted on us, and believe me, they did, Mum and Dad always made time for each other. When we were old enough to look after ourselves, they'd go away for weekends, go to concerts, and even have date nights.

Their relationship is the goal for me. I know that now. It's strange when you're a kid to think of your parents as anything but the people who are supposed to love and care for you. It was only when I was in my teens and heard some of their stories, that I realised they were and still are their own people. It's probably why we're all so close as adults. Although I could have done without hearing *some* of the stories to be honest.

So, even when Beth and I move closer to Hebden, I know Mum and Dad will still have their own lives. It will probably take Mum a few months to get all that mothering out of the way, but I know she will. I'm guessing a few Sunday dinners with all three grown kids bickering will pave the way. I can't wait.

Beth is completely lost in the land of weddings. Morgan looks amused, but bored. To be fair, I can handle about ten minutes of wedding planning before I'm ready to tear my hair out. Mum keeps flitting over to us to add her penny's worth. I'm close to asking if I can help behind the till just to escape.

"Are you ready to go?" Niamh asks moments later. Maybe she could sense my brain melting.

"God, yes." Clearing my throat, I wait for Beth to stop yammering on about flower arrangements. "We're off. Places to go, and all that."

"Don't think this gets you out of planning with me, Nic."

I feign innocence. "I'd never think that. God, what do you take me for, little sister?"

"I take you for a sibling that detests anything to do with wedding planning and will use every opportunity to get out of it."

"That's fair," I admit. "But...we have Christmas-related things to be thinking of before your nuptials."

Beth nods. "Speaking of, we need to debrief."

"Later. I've got some skating to do."

"Ah, you're off, love?" Mum asks as she returns to the table for the millionth time.

"Yeah. We'll see you later."

Her eyes dance between me and Niamh. "Have fun, you two. Don't do anything I wouldn't do."

I don't even want to pull on that conversational thread, so I scoop Niamh's hand into mine and practically frog-march her out of the shop. The ice rink is only a short walk away. The council set it up in the car park opposite the town hall. It's already getting darker, even though it's just past midday. That bodes well for me because the lights will come on soon, and that will absolutely make this date a hundred times more romantic.

It's a Saturday, so the rink and general area will be a lot busier, but there's not a great deal I can do about it. If I had a lot more money, I would've looked into hiring out the entire rink, but that's not the case, so I'll have to make do. Should I have brought flowers? No, that would be impractical. God, I suck at this.

"You're lookin' mighty pensive, Nic."

I flush, but don't turn away. "I was just thinking of all the things I could have done to make the date more memorable."

"Oh, and what did you come up with?"

We're still holding hands. Just like we did at the market. I like the feel. She fits with me. "Oh, if I'd had the money to rent the whole rink. Or if I should've bought flowers."

"As sweet as those thoughts are, you don't need to worry. The date is already great."

"We haven't done anything yet." I laugh.

"We're hanging out together. Isn't that enough?"

"Cheesy," I reply, grinning.

"Heard it and owning it," she shoots back.

The lights come on, casting the whole town in a warm glow of red and gold. Thanking the weather gods for the cloud cover, I pull her close to me and wrap my arm around her waist as we walk. My nerves kick in when I realise this date has the potential to end in disaster. I don't mean emotionally. I mean physical, bodily harm. I'm not a novice on the ice, but I'm not Torvill or Dean either. I lamely promised to catch Niamh if she falls, but I'm thinking that could end us both up in A&E.

"So, when was the last time you did this?" Gesturing my head to the rink. There is already a decent-size line by the ticket booth.

"Last year. I went with a few friends."

"So, you're not terrible then?"

She shrugs her shoulders. We queue up like good British people. Our conversation is light and easy. As always. The poor girl at the ticket booth looks a few seconds away from a meltdown. Not all customers are nice ones, and I bet she's had some arses to deal with. I give her a wide smile. I think my reindeer bobble hat helps. It has fluffy ears. She gives me a smirk and carries out our ticket transaction.

I'm no germaphobe, but I really struggle with public sharing, i.e. putting my foot in a skate that someone else has just worn. It's still warm. Niamh laughs when she sees my face all scrunched up. "You're too cute," she mumbles, while continuing without a problem to slip her feet into her boots.

I'd rather not worry about athlete's foot than look cute, but whatever. We walk-slash-hobble to the rink entrance. Being the gentlewoman I am, I step aside to let Niamh enter the ice first. She rolls her eyes at me, to let me know she thinks I'm a dork. I think it was the little bow I did as she went by that solidified it.

Niamh holds onto the railings as I step through the little gate. It takes me a second, but I finally get my balance. I'm sure I still resemble Bambi, but it doesn't matter. I know I can skate in circles well enough to make this date fun. And if Niamh does need me to hold her up, then I'll do my best to make it as romantic as possible.

Turns out, she doesn't need my help in the slightest. The second I see her push away from the barrier with the grace of a ballerina, I know she's been pulling my leg. If anyone might need catching, it's me. Niamh is a winter dream on skates. I'm momentarily mesmerised as I watch her long, dark hair whip behind her as she moves. Her legs are strong and showcase very toned muscles as she pushes off. I, on the other hand, stumble after her with the grace of a tea bag.

"You lied," I call after her retreating yummy bum. God, those jeans are wonderful.

"I didn't lie." She grins, looking over her shoulder. Just to rub it in a bit more, she spins around so she's skating backwards.

"You were all like 'I can't promise I'll stay on my feet a lot,' and I said something cheesy."

"At no point did I say it would be from lack of talent on the ice that I'd find myself on the floor. I was referring to how delicious you look in your winter gear. Makes me weak at the knees, Nic."

Oh, she's smooth!

# December 22nd

"What the bloody hell happened to you, love?" Dad looks suitably alarmed as I stare at him from the couch, where I have been wedged face down since last night.

Niamh wanted to stay, but my humiliation won out and I kindly asked her to leave me alone. I don't think she was offended. God, I hope not. But I couldn't break down with her in the same room. We're not at that point in our friendship-slash-relationship yet.

However, I think my mortification was warranted. I'm sure Niamh has never been on a date where the person she's with has been taken out by a two-foot penguin to the tune of *I Saw Mommy Kissing Santa Claus* before. At least I'll always be memorable to her. I wouldn't be surprised if she declines a second date. It's truly unbelievable how clumsy and idiotic I am around her. I should invite her on a work ride along with me, so she actually gets the chance to see I'm a fully functioning and capable woman. Not sure my new boss would approve, but I'm willing to risk it at this stage.

Oh, let's not forget my best friend caught it all on camera. I should have foreseen it! Tammy is hellbent on revenge after my—hilarious—Tammy Face Plant montage. I bet she's been stalking me, getting ready to pounce.

"Do you need me to run you down to A&E?" Dad is squatting next to me. I'm lying on my front, because my coccyx bone is sending out warning signals that if I even attempt to place any pressure on it, I will be deeply sorry.

"Maybe Urgent Care rather than A&E, I'm not dying." I'd feel awful taking up room in A&E for a bruised bottom.

"No, she's just got a pain in her arse." Beth chuckles, walking in with a fresh coffee.

"Yeah, it's short with red frizzy hair," I shoot back.

"Oh, good one, sis," she tuts. "So original."

"You two are terrible. It's like being transported back to the worst time in your childhoods," Dad says.

Harsh.

"Do you want an ice pack?" Beth asks, signalling a ceasefire.

"Yes, please." I groan when Morgan, Ted, Liam, and Mum walk in. Tammy is suspiciously absent. Probably editing and uploading that damn footage.

"I did a year in medical school before deciding it wasn't for me," Morgan says brightly. "Do you want me to take a look?"

"Why the hell not," I say, resigned to the familial audience, making themselves comfy around me.

"Here, love, have some eggnog. It's the good stuff," Mum murmurs close to my ear. We'll bypass the fact it's only 9:52 a.m. I take the proffered mug and take generous pulls from the candy cane straw. Wowzer, she wasn't kidding. That's some strong-ass nog!

"Alright, let's take a look." Morgan gingerly moves my sweatpants and peeks in my boxers. I can't even begin to explain how painful it was to change last night. A few hisses and expletives escape my mouth as she pokes and prods.

"I don't think it's broken. Just bruised, which is still super painful. An x-ray would confirm."

"I'll call Michael and see if he's working today," Mum says, like I should know who the bloody hell Michael is.

"Keep the ice on it and take painkillers. I think you'll be fine in a couple of days. It might be that you jarred your back when you hit the floor, which is adding to your discomfort."

"Thanks," I say, turning to look at a smiley Morgan.

"We're in luck. Michael is on duty. He'll get us sorted," Mum announces to the room. I'm still none the wiser, but whatever. If this Michael can help, I'll be his number one fan.

Asking my family why they all feel the need to come along with me to get my arse x-rayed was pointless. There was just a bunch of noise and everyone putting their coats and scarfs on.

As I take a small step out of the house, I look up into the arresting eyes of Niamh, who by all accounts was about to knock on the front door.

"Hi," I say with my arm slung over Dad's shoulder. I tried to explain it was my bum that hurt, not my legs, but my words fell on deaf ears.

"Where are you going?" She steps forward and cups my face. In plain sight of everyone. "Are you really hurt?"

Her concern is sweet, but I don't want her to worry too much.

I feel daft now, sending her away yesterday. "Thought it might be best to get checked out."

She nods her head while her eyes take in the other five people standing around. "I'll take you," she says, to everyone's surprise. "No offence, but Nic doesn't need you all there. And it was my fault she got hurt, so I'll nip her down."

"Are you sure, love?" Dad asks. Mum is quietly watching the exchange. She tends to go into Mother Hen mode when one of us is sick or injured, but she's keeping a lid on it for now.

"Absolutely. Beth, will you run up and grab an overnight bag for her? We'll go straight back to mine afterwards, if that's okay?" Her eyes are back on me.

"That sounds great," I croak. I don't know why I'm suddenly feeling emotional.

"Alright you lot, back in the house," Mum calls. "Let us know how she goes, won't you, sweetheart?"

Niamh smiles. "Of course. I'll message you as soon as I know anything."

Beth arrives seconds later with my holdall. "You could have brought some nice underwear, Nic," she tuts. I roll my eyes.

I'll ignore that dig. My boxers are great. Niamh certainly appreciates them. "Bye, Beth."

Sending a wink my way, she cuffs me on the shoulder. "See ya. I'll tell Tammy to hold off on the screening until you're back home."

Niamh chuckles and moves me before I can start anything. "Let's go."

I've never been more uncomfortable sitting in a car. Every bump sends a shooting pain up from my arse to my back. I see Niamh wince every time I gasp. We make it to the Urgent Care unit relatively unscathed. Niamh was a true hero. She slowed way down when she saw bumps or potholes. Her Irish flare certainly peeped out when a driver got a little heated. Niamh belted out a string of words that were so heavily accented I couldn't make them all out, but I got the gist that the guy she was swearing at probably needed to go to a shaman or something, if he ever wanted to live a normal curse free life again. There was something about his genitals and never knowing pleasure again. Poor guy.

"You must be Nicole," a very tall and buff man asks as we enter the waiting room.

"She is," Niamh answers because I'm too busy looking up at this giant of a human.

"I'm Michael. Your mum phoned ahead. Luckily, we're not too busy, which is a miracle at this time of year."

"Um, okay." My bum hurts, and now my neck is aching as I look up at him. How the ruddy hell does Mum know Michael?

"We just need to fill in some details and then I'll get you taken down to x-ray."

He's very to-the-point, which I appreciate. "So, how do you know, Mum?" I ask in between answering medical questions.

"Oh, I started volunteering at the LGBTQIA+ centre a few months ago. Your mum set me up with my boyfriend." He grins.

"Sounds like her." I smile. "Do you enjoy volunteering?"

"Yes, I wish I could do more, but my shifts are erratic, and honestly, I'm bloody knackered most of the time. Richard, my fella, gets to spend more time there than me. He's a freelance editor. Lucky bugger."

"Hey, you should pop into the tea shop next time you're around," Niamh says, her hand on my knee. "I'll slip a scone in for free."

"I'll never turn down a free scone. It's a date. Richard has been nagging at me to make more friends. You'd think we'd been married for decades the way we are with each other," he titters.

"Sometimes you just know when someone is right," Niamh comments. I'm trying, once again, not to get ahead of myself. But I hope she's referring to me when she says things like that. I sure feel right with her.

"Right, I'm going to have to ask you to wait here for a little while," Michael says to Niamh. "She won't be too long."

Niamh stands from her chair and bends down to kiss me tenderly. "See you soon."

"Mmmhmm." I'm grinning like an idiot. I can feel it. Michael gives me a sweet smile. He whisks me away seconds later.

"You two are sweet. Your mum was right. She told me you'd make an exceptional couple."

"Glad she filled you in." I laugh.

The radiologist is a woman in her late fifties with a strong Yorkshire accent. She gets me situated without fuss or conversation, which is fine by me. I think Niamh's kisses have healing powers, because I'm already feeling much better. The result of the x-ray is negative for a break. I'll need to be careful sitting for a few days, but that's it. Phew, Christmas isn't ruined.

Niamh collects me and wheels me back to my car as soon as I'm released. She's got a bag with her which is curious. "Don't get excited," she says when I peer into it the moment I'm sitting in the passenger seat. "It's a donut."

"Oh, I love doughnuts."

Her laughter seems out of place. "It's a donut for your bum, babe."

Well, that's disappointing.

The bum donut turned out to be less disappointing than I first thought. Settled on Niamh's sofa next to an open fire with twinkly lights, hopped up on pain meds is actually quite delightful. The donut is making it easy to get comfortable. Now, I just need Niamh to stop stressing and sit down with me. I'm not sure why she's in such a tizzy.

"Will you park your arse down," I finally say after watching her buzz around the cottage.

"Sorry, I just want everything to be perfect."

"What for? Are you about to propose to me, Niamh O'Conner? I have to say it's a little early."

My grin earns me a flick on the nose. "No, you eejit. I thought this could be our second date. If you feel up to it. No problem if not."

Smiling at her nervousness, I reach over and stroke her hand. "What did you have in mind?"

"Christmas movie marathon, of course. I have hot chocolate. Popcorn, and mince pies."

"With very little chance of someone breaking their arse. Sounds like a winning date plan to me."

She scoots closer. "I am sorry about that. If I'd known you were about to get ploughed by a hyperactive toddler with a plastic penguin, I wouldn't have distracted you by flirting."

I scoff. "Pfft, totally worth it. I love it when you flirt."

We smile at each other, and then Niamh leans forward and plants a deliciously sensual kiss on me. "Are you sure a movie night is worthy of being called a date?"

"Stop worrying. This is perfect. Something you should know. I'm not looking for glitz and glamour. I want the nights in, snuggled on the sofa watching favourite films. I want to take snowy walks, and then stop for a pint, while all the time holding hands. Is...is that what you are looking for?"

To my relief, Niamh smiles and nods her head. "Yes. I want all of that. But mostly I want to feel safe and loved."

Swallowing hard, I shift just enough for my bum to let me know of its displeasure. But I won't let a bruised tailbone stop me now. "I want to make you feel those things, if you'll let me, Niamh. I know we need to take things slowly, and I'm more than happy to do that. I just want you to know that I'll treasure whatever you give me, like I treasure this time of year with my family."

I watch as she gently bites her lips. "I don't know how you've not been snapped up, Nicole. You're the whole package, wrapped up in a beautifully strong body."

That makes me laugh. "Not everyone wants this kind of package."

"Well, I do."

"Then, let's keep doing what we're doing, and see what happens."

"Would…would it be okay if I spent Christmas Eve with you? I know you'll need to be at your parents', but I'd like to be with you if that's okay?"

"I'd love that. What about your mum?"

Niamh huffs. "Well, Mum's decided to bugger off on a cruise. She leaves tomorrow for a week!"

"All the better for me." I smile, nipping her bottom lip. "And, yes, I need to be at home on Christmas Eve. Liam would never forgive me if I weren't. But until then, I'm happy to be here with you. A little alone time is nice."

"Won't your mum be upset? She loves having you all home."

I shrug. "I'll be around permanently soon. I think she's just happy I'm here. And if I had to guess, the fact you and I are spending so much time together is probably the cherry on the top for her this year."

She leans forward again and brushes her nose against mine. "It's been the cherry on top for me, too."

If I had a little less pain, I would gladly take this to the next level, but maybe simply being here together, talking and existing is what we need. I'm done opening calendar doors. If Niamh is willing to do this with me, I'm all in.

# December 23rd

I heard them! I know I did. But it's far too early. The bells have never chimed before nightfall. There I go, sounding like bloody Beth. Putting aside my Victorian ramblings, it's still true. The sleigh bells only ring in the evening. And yet, here I am sitting bolt upright in Niamh's bed because I heard the fuckers! And it's 7:30 a.m.

Maybe it's a Pavlov's Dog kind of thing. Mum's got us so well-trained that when we hear anything resembling a bell, we instantly react. At least I'm not salivating. Niamh is still out of it, so they couldn't have been loud. If they really rang at all. It could have been a dream. Laying my head down on the pillow, I snuggle up to Niamh. She's wearing penguins in snowsuits nightwear, and I'm so for it. She looks adorable.

I'm just taking a second whiff of Niamh's skin when I hear them, plain as day! I'm out of bed in a snap. Hobbling straight to the window, I throw them open, disregarding it's like the chuffing North Pole out there. My nipples could cut glass right now. The landscape is still a snow-covered wonderland. More of the white stuff seems to have fallen overnight. Niamh's bedroom faces the front of the property, giving me a great viewpoint over her front garden. There are no tracks suggesting anyone came by last night.

Lurching out of the bedroom, I go to the bathroom, which is at the back of the property, and throw open that window too. I've inadvertently created a polar vortex of wind. Shoving my head out into the bracing cold, I look over the back garden. Nothing but pure, untouched snow.

"What the hell are you doing?" Niamh calls, rushing into the bathroom, her fleece robe wrapped tightly around her body. She doesn't look happy. "Why have I just been woken by the freezing wind howling through my bedroom?"

"Um...bells, I heard bells."

"And you needed to turn us into snow people, because?"

"I..." Shit. This is where my Christmas fairytale is about to unravel.

Her shoulders drop, and she seems to be calming down a fraction. "You were checking the garden for track marks, right?" I nod stupidly, waiting for her to lose it, and kick me out. "Next time, will ya try to remember to close one window before opening another?" A few more stupid nods from me, and Niamh is satisfied enough to give me a peck on the cheek before heading back to the bedroom.

Turning slowly, I shut the bathroom window. That overly emotional feeling is back. Why didn't Niamh get more upset? Knowing I'm never going to get back to sleep, I limp to the kitchen. I'm going to whip up a feast for Niamh, in a way of saying thank you. Which is odd, I guess. What am I saying thank you for? Not shouting at me or telling me the sleigh bells are stupid. Not getting frustrated with my lack of thought? Well, all of that, to be honest. She's the first woman I've been with who hasn't done one or all of those things.

I'm going to make her almond and honey porridge with a side of muesli, topped with strawberries and chocolate shavings. A good pot of tea and coffee, so she can choose. Damn, I should have nipped to the shop and bought some of those oven-ready croissants. Never mind, I don't want to risk leaving and Niamh wake up to find me gone. Rooting around her cupboards, I find some pre-made waffles. Might as well add them, too.

The kitchen will need a damn good clean. Not entirely sure how I made such a mess, considering the only thing I had to make was the porridge. The rest just needed heating and popping on the tray.

Tip toeing back to the bedroom, I lay the tray on the end of the bed as gently as possible. Niamh is fast asleep again. And she is so beautiful, my chest hurts. She's still no graceful sleeper. Her hair is once again across her face and in her mouth. A hand is thrown above her head, and she's snoring.

I realise my ass is hardly hurting now I've been up and moving about for a while. The donut, plus Niamh's attention, has cured me. I think she could make anything feel better with just a little of her time. So cheesy! And, oh my god, I just realised I *am* in the middle of a Hallmark Christmas movie. Just without the heteronormativity. I mean, think about it. I've come back to my small-ish town looking for a break after a string of failed relationships and feeling like I need a change, only to have met and fallen for my brother's best friend. You could literally write this shit and sell it to a movie producer. I'll add that to my list of things to do after I've got my life in order.

Okay, time to do some thanking. Shifting up the bed, I sit next to Niamh. Using the tips of my fingers, I brush her hair away and pick the rest out of her mouth. Her eyes flutter momentarily, but that's followed by a snort as she rolls on her side away from me.

Chuckling, I move the collar of her sleep shirt out of the way and kiss her shoulder. I get all the way to her earlobe before she reacts. It's not a sexy mewl, or groan. No, she bats me straight in the face, and grunts.

Time to take things up a notch. I bite down gently on her earlobe, and snake my hand across her torso, tracing patterns up and around her boobs. Finally, I get a contented sigh. "Hey…" She hums sleepily.

"Good morning, lovely lady. I made breakfast."

"But I was sleeping," she moans.

"There's porridge and waffles, and other stuff."

Turning on her back, she stretches and finally opens her eyes. "What's the occasion?"

"No occasion. Just because…" I don't want to tell her I was so overwhelmed with her being perfectly perfect for me, I felt the need to cook up a storm to say thank you. "And look, what else I found." Holding up a plastic sprig of mistletoe, I give her my best wink.

"Oh, well, that makes waking up worth it, then." She's so much better at flirting than me, but that's cool. I don't mind being close to forty and crap at flirting if it works for Niamh. "C'mere."

Our chemistry has always been sky-high, and usually it leads to fast, hard, and lustful sex. This kiss, the one we're sharing right now, feels like it's leading to more than sex. So far, I've had several moments where this feeling swirled in my chest and has made me feel like the relationship building between us is more than sex. It really feels like this could be the one. *She* feels like the one, and that's scary as hell.

Her hands trail through my hair, but the caress is missing its usual sexual and—appreciated—aggression. Her fingers find their way to my face. Pulling back slightly, I leave my lips with a whisper of a space from hers. Our eyes meet, and I know for sure, she's feeling the magic.

I want to take my time and let all these feelings channel through to her. I shift so I can peel back the duvet. She's so warm when I lower myself on top. Her legs open, letting me sink into her. Instead of rolling my hips, I spend minutes kissing her, letting my hands discover her body in a way that is new to us both. Niamh cups my face again, like she's holding something delicate and breakable.

Our breaths quicken as we fall deeper into each other. This is possibly the first time we've been horizontal while having sex. Correction—and this is beyond gag-worthy—this isn't just the first time we're horizontal; it's the first time we're making love.

I feel the waistband of Niamh's sleep trousers under my fingers, so I take the opportunity to push them down. Niamh lifts to allow the material to be moved. There's a brief pause while Niamh kicks them to the bottom of the bed. Her hands find my boxers. Our lips haven't left each other, and I can't get enough. Wiggling out of my boxers, I can't keep the moan in as our bodies meet again, skin on skin. My hands run up her ribs, taking her t-shirt as they ascend. Niamh wastes no time sitting up and allowing me to take her top up and over her head. Her hair looks gorgeous as it cascades back down from the neck of her top. If it's possible, her eyes seem to shine even brighter than usual, but that could just be me.

My tank top lands somewhere to the side of me. The feel of her bare breasts on mine is beyond amazing. There isn't an inch of space between us when I finally rock myself into her. We are both wet, evidenced by the slickness I feel between us. Every movement is slow and precise. The heat building is not in the physical sense. It's internal and combustible. My clit is so hard, a couple of strong rubs and I will be falling over the edge. But the pressure isn't strong. It's unbelievably gentle, and feels epically good. Like I can sense the orgasm building is about to undo me.

Niamh's hand settles at the base of my neck. Her mouth is open slightly as her breath hitches. Planting my hands on either side of her head, I roll deeper. "Look at me," I gasp. I want to see those emerald eyes shine brighter than the sun as she comes.

"Nic. Oh!"

"Stay with me," I manage to rasp out as the wave that has been slowly building begins to peak. I want to close my eyes and bask in its all-encompassing power. But the pull of Niamh is greater, and she is looking straight at me as I push harder one more time, and I see the millisecond Niamh's orgasm takes her. Her moan is swallowed by silence as her eyes widen, still looking at me. Her eyebrows crease as our bodies tremble to the point of vibration. My fists are white as I grip the pillow under her head, and our shared pleasure surges between us.

The pressure I feel around my back pulls me back to the present. Niamh has pulled me close, her head buried in my neck as we try to regulate our bodies and breathing.

The banter that usually follows is also missing. I think we're both taking a second to let what just happened settle. My mind suddenly jumps to the breakfast. "You didn't get to eat your porridge."

Her laugh booms around the room. "That's what you want to say after what we just did?"

"Um...no, not at all," I whine, utterly bamboozled by my mouth's betrayal.

She's still laughing. "I should think not. I mean, that was...different, right?" Her voice is quieter, and I know she's feeling vulnerable.

"It was different, and amazing," I say, leaning back down to kiss her nose.

"We're really doing this, aren't we?" she asks. I don't have time to respond. "Because I want us to be doing this, Nic. I'm in this. Sleigh bells and all."

"Sleigh bells and all. That's what she said?" Tammy asks through mouthfuls of ice cream. She was watching television in my room when I came home. I eventually tore myself away from Niamh. It wasn't my choice, but she had a shift at the tea shop. It worked out well, because I realised I needed to talk things through with Tammy after this morning's activities and feelings.

"Yes, those were her words."

"So, what's with the panicked look?"

"Tam, you have..." I wave my hand in front of her face. Did she just shove her head in the tub?

"I'll get it in a minute. Come on, this is what you want, right?" Tammy makes no effort to wipe her face, so I try to move on and not let it distract me.

"I want to know it's really real, you know. We're in a Christmas fairytale right now, and I guess it freaks me out to think of what happens after the twenty-fifth. When I have to go back down south and pack up my life, who's to say the space won't give Niamh time to think and change her mind? It's not all gingerbread-making and ice skating."

"Or climbing roofs."

"Well, that happens more often than not in our line of work." I grin.

"Huh, yeah. Well, not for me anymore. I'm just going to sit and get fat, then pop out a baby."

"Yeah, you are, and it's going to be amazing."

"Back to you." Tammy points. "I think this is the result of seventeen wrong women getting in your head. For the first time ever, I can tell you categorically that Niamh is a good woman, and she's in this."

"You never actually told me what was said between the two of you," I say, squinting my eyes, trying to look accusing.

Tammy rolls her eyes. "First and foremost, I said I'd kick her bum back to Ireland if she hurt you."

"Tammy!"

"Relax, I didn't, really. I wanted to know the real reason behind the whole Pat stunt. I knew there was more to it than Niamh being a shitty player."

"What made you think that?"

"Just a hunch. Plus, I saw how she looked at you, Nic. The admiration is entirely mutual."

I blow out a breath. "Maybe that's what's throwing me, Tammy. Knowing she's someone I can actually see myself growing old with. And let's not forget it's been ten years since I saw her, and only twenty-odd days since reconnecting."

She blows a raspberry. "The time isn't important. It's the feelings that matter. Talk to her and keep on talking until your insecurities and worries are put to rest. Don't fuck this up, Nicole. I mean, shit, she literally loves the idea of spending time with your family looking for imaginary sleigh bells. She's your person."

"Hey, they're not imaginary!"

She cocks her eyebrow. "Are you sure?

# Christmas Eve

"That is one snappy jumper you're sporting there, Nic!" Mum holds my arms out so she can get a proper look. I went all out this year. "Is that your squad?"

Smiling, I nod. "Yeah. I found a woman who offered personalised knitting patterns. Look, there's Tammy, falling over a fire extinguisher. Roberts stuck up a tree. Spencer eating all the turkey."

Mum throws back her head, laughing. "I think you're in prime position for this year's Christmas Jumper Competition."

"Right! I'm going to take the title this year."

"Nic, look at my Hulk jumper," Liam cries, bounding in with a happy-looking Reggie tucked under his arm.

"Looking good, little bro!"

"I went with Elsa this year," Beth says as she enters the living room. Ted has his usual Star Wars jumper on. Morgan's is multicoloured and not entirely Christmas-themed, but that's cool. "Where is Tammy?"

"I'm here, and look, I even made an effort." I can't help but laugh when I see her Grinch jumper. Tammy acts like she's not a Christmas-y person, but it's all lies. She loves this shit as much as the rest of us.

"You all look great," Mum coos. "What time is Niamh getting here, Nic?"

"Anytime. Has Dad gone to fetch Aileen and Wally?"

"Yes, so let's use the time to get the table set. You know how I like it, so please don't argue."

We're like a well-oiled machine after all this time. I take on the napkins, shaping them into Pope's hats. Beth will lay out the cutlery and glassware. Liam is on plates and Christmas crackers. And Ted will walk 'round, pretending to check on our work, but really he steals the snacks from the side table. Morgan is already out the door as she needs to visit Betsy.

The front door opens to a cacophony of happy voices. Aileen is laughing at something my dad has said. And then I hear the voice I've been waiting for all day. Niamh. Although she didn't have work today, she had to tend to some things at her mum's place. I asked her to pack a bag for a couple of days, because I don't want to lose any time with her. It's only two days, and then I will have to head south to start sorting my life out.

"Hey there, sexy lady," Niamh calls as she comes into the living room. Everyone stops and stares as I heat up. We've been pretty low-key, I think, but obviously Niamh doesn't feel the need now we are giving the relationship a real go. Striding over in a long Christmas jumper dress that has sparkly snowflakes, Niamh stops in front of me and places an unrushed kiss on my lips. Once she's rendered me mute, Niamh pulls away with a wink. "So, how can I help?"

My family is smiling from ear to ear, which I should be happy about, but I'm feeling too embarrassed by how affected I am. The woman only has to look at me, and I'm a gooey mess.

"No, love, nothing to do," Mum calls from the doorway. "Why don't we all have a drink? It's not every year we have such a full house."

I take the opportunity to gather myself by fetching two bottles of champagne from the fridge. Liam holds his hands against his ears as we pop the corks. He always has a Buck's Fizz. Although he's old enough to drink, he's not a huge fan of alcohol.

Dad raises his flute. "Here's to another wonderful December spent with the people we love. Including our wonderful new additions. Morgan, you're welcome anytime. Niamh, I hope this is the first of many family traditions you'll be a part of. Merry Christmas!"

We all go to cheer, but Mum stops us. "Just one last thing. I know it's your dad's thing to do the toast, but I wanted to say how happy I am that we still do this every year. We are the luckiest parents in the world, and I can't tell you how excited I am to have Nic, Beth, and Tammy move closer to home. I'm finally going to be a grandma. Hopefully Beth and Ted won't keep me waiting for a second set of tiny feet to cherish."

"Jeez, Mum, relax, we're not even married yet. Anyway, what about Nic and Nim? They might beat us to it."

"Hey, don't drag us into it." I laugh.

Tammy starts sobbing. "You guys are the best," she cries, tackling Mum. Her hormones seem to be on a rollercoaster ride at the minute. Mum just chuckles and holds her tight.

"I don't want babies," Liam announces. "I'd prefer a new Xbox."

"Here, here," Wally calls, draining his drink, earning him a soft hit to the gut from Aileen.

"Well, that was interesting," Morgan says from the back.

"Okay folks. We have a good hour and a half before the turkey is done. Shall we go for a pint?"

There's a collective cheer of yes. We always go to the pub for a drink before sitting down for Christmas dinner. We're just about to leave the house when the landline rings. Mum picks it up. "Liam, it's for you, sweetheart."

We're all crowded in the hallway dressed in big coats and scarfs. Liam clears a path through us all. Niamh stands next to me and slips her hand in mine. We watch Liam take the phone from Mum. Beth and I know what is about to happen and it makes my eyes water. Liam's face lights up as he talks. He nods and chatters while looking at us with wide eyes. Finally, he presses the red disconnect button. He is almost shaking with excitement.

"Everything all right, lad?" Dad asks.

"You won't believe who that was," he begins. I can hear the disbelief and wonder in his voice. "That... That was Santa," he whispers. "The real one!"

"Oh my god, really?" Beth chimes in. I remember the first time Santa called me. That thirty-second phone call made my entire year. Mum and Dad stopped them when we all reached double digits, but the year Liam had his accident, the phone calls started again. And every year since, he's just as surprised and excited. It's beautiful to see. I wish all adults could keep hold of their innocence and childlike wonder.

"Tell us on the way to the pub, love," Mum calls over the crowd, pushing us out the door.

The Black Sheep is packed when we arrive. Everyone is in a good mood, cheering new patrons as they walk through the door. Mum always has the forethought to reserve a table for us. We take several minutes to get through all the well-wishers. I'm surprised how many women try to corral Niamh into giving them a kiss under strategically placed mistletoe. I'm guessing my face gives away the fact I'm not happy because after the third, yes *third* woman, who tries to steal a kiss from my girlfriend, Niamh laughs at me but pulls me tight to her body and plants the perfect kiss on me.

If that doesn't let everyone know Niamh is off the market, I don't know what will.

"Since when is Hebden a hive of thirsty sapphics," I grumble after she's finished snogging my face off.

"The drinks are flowing, that's all. No need to go all brooding girlfriend on me."

"So, we are...girlfriends, right?"

She plants another kiss on me. "Yes, Nic. We are. Now come on, we've got a Christmas Eve tradition to get to."

"Oh my god, that turkey smells amazing," Tammy says the second the front door opens. And to be fair, she's not wrong. I cannot wait to dig into Christmas dinner. Mum makes the best roast potatoes on the planet. Plus, the stuffing balls that are cooked in goose fat. Oh, yeah, it's the best dinner ever.

"Okay, battle stations," Mum shouts. Dad takes a tipsy Wally and sits him down. Aileen follows Mum into the kitchen, where they will dish up and do many wonderful things to make the dinner perfect. I pour drinks at one end of the table, while Beth does the other end. Niamh and Morgan stand on one side of the dining room, looking uncertain. I take Niamh by the hand and guide her to her seat. Then I point to the one set for Morgan. "Just sit down and enjoy a drink. We've got this."

Liam comes from his bedroom where he lets us all know that Reggie is happily chewing on a bone and therefore won't be a pain in the bum all night. Tammy is... I have no idea, but I'll guess she followed the food smells.

Minutes later, we get the order to sit in our designated spots. I'm next to Niamh and, for the first time ever, I'm completely content. I'm sitting here with my family and my girlfriend. Mum and Aileen dish up, and Dad carves the turkey. Not out of any misguided gender role expectations. Just because he's the only one who so far hasn't caused injury to themselves while doing it.

Mum passes me the potatoes first, therefore telling me I'm clearly her favourite child. Liam goes to town on the mash, and Beth hoards the pigs in blankets. It's only when I catch sight of Tammy and Niamh chuckling that I stop my potato grab.

"Are you lot always like this?" By you lot, I think Niamh is referring to us Robinson kids.

"Um..."

"Yes, they are," Aileen interrupts. "Nothing comes between them and their Christmas dinner. Take note. If there is ever a time Linda can't cook, you need to know what's expected."

Mum scoffs. "Never. I'll be doing this for a long time, although I'm happy to teach anyone who would like to learn."

"I'm in," Niamh says. "These Brussels are amazing. Plus, I should learn how to keep this one happy." She grins. My face heats. Again.

"And what exactly is Nic doing to keep *you* happy?" Beth shoots. I'm not sure if she meant to ask a question that has a very inappropriate answer, but everyone at the table apart from Liam grows quiet.

Niamh clears her throat. "She makes excellent porridge." I burst out laughing because it's so ridiculous.

Mum chuckles. "She takes after me. I make great porridge, don't I love?" Dad looks as mortified as me and mumbles something, causing Mum and Aileen to cackle.

"Why are we talking about porridge? It's Christmas dinner time," Liam pipes up, thankfully giving me a reason to change the subject.

"Hey, we need to pull crackers!"

"Nicole, you are absolutely right," Mum agrees, already picking up her party cracker. In a flurry of movement, several cracks echo through the room. Nothing screams Christmas like grown adults sitting at the dinner table in paper hats and playing with crap toys.

With the crackers pulled, the turkey eaten, and Wally asleep in a food coma, the family moves away from the table to begin the epic cleanup. "Nic, can I just borrow you for a second?" Niamh asks me. I look at Mum. She works really hard and I don't want to just abandon her; especially when Beth and Dad are about as useful as a chocolate teapot where cleaning is concerned.

"Go, love. We'll be fine."

Smiling, I take Niamh's hand and let her pull me out of the dining room and down to the War Room. The fairy lights are already lit, and there is soft music playing. If I didn't know any better, I'd say Niamh O'Conner is trying to seduce me. "My, this is cosy," I comment. Niamh turns and pulls me close. The kiss isn't unexpected, but the intensity we work up to in such a short amount of time is.

My hand snakes up Niamh's thigh, gradually taking her jumper dress higher and higher. I am seconds from touching Niamh where I so desperately want to when the door flies open and Beth and Liam come running down the stairs.

"I hope you're both decent," Beth shouts.

"I'm gonna kill her," I growl. Niamh laughs.

She readjusts her dress and kisses me on the lips. "Later."

"Tonight is the last night," Liam says, brushing past us to sit on the sofa.

Beth leans against the wall. "He's right, Nic. One more night to find those bloody bells."

"I'm surprised we haven't heard them by now," I comment. "Oh shit, I forgot to tell you about yesterday morning!" I spend a few minutes updating them on my bell experience at Niamh's.

"That's a new one!" Beth declares, marching over to the map and marking a new spot right over Niamh's cottage. "She's gone off plan."

"I just don't see how it's possible," I say.

"What if we don't hear the bells tonight? Does that mean Santa won't come?" Liam asks.

Niamh clamps a hand on his shoulder. "You spoke to him earlier, Li. He said you had to be asleep early tonight, didn't he?"

"Yeah, that's true."

315

Crisis averted.

"Okay, I'm going to ask Ted to take a walk with me. Maybe we can get lucky."

I nod. "Take Morgan. She can walk Betsy, and that's one more set of eyes."

Beth claps. That's her way of solidifying a decision. "Liam, you need to get ready for bed, buddy."

"Okay. But tomorrow, I'm staying up with you guys."

"Obviously," I say.

"Yes! Nim, you'll be here too, right?"

"I will."

Liam rushes over and hugs us both, then bolts up the stairs. "Okay, you two," Beth says, waving her hand between Niamh and me, "can get back to whatever it was you were doing."

"Goodbye, Beth. Tell Mum I'll be up soon to help wash the dishes."

"Such a good daughter," Beth mocks. She skips up the stairs before I have time to retort.

As soon as the door closes, I turn to Niamh, hoping we can pick up where we left off. AKA, my hand up her dress. "Hold that thought," Niamh says, stopping me mid-step. "Come here," she adds, reaching for my hand.

Instead of pulling me closer and kissing me, she walks me over to the calendar.

"Um...please don't tell me I have to open another door." I try to say it jokingly, but a part of me is suddenly not feeling so confident and it's making the food in my stomach curdle.

Niamh cups my face, and I've decided that's my new favourite thing she does. "Relax. I'm hoping after this you'll never open another one of those stupid doors ever again." I swallow. "Nicole, I thought it would take me years to be ready for the level of commitment I want with you. After yesterday, my mind finally caught up with my heart. Now, I'm not saying I'm ready to say those three words, or anything. But, I know that I will. And I wanted to be open with you about that. If...if you don't think that's where you can see us, let's talk it out now. Because I was serious yesterday, Nic. I'm completely in this. And I get that we've had a bit of a Christmas fairytale time of it. But I know I'm still going to want this after tomorrow, and through all the other months of the year."

"I want that," I choke out before taking her lips with mine. I move close to her and let our bodies connect fully. My tongue brushes against hers and I'm ready to confess exactly what I feel when I hear them. That gentle jingle. But instead of pulling away, I continue to kiss this wonderful woman.

Niamh pushes me back, looking confused. "You heard that, right?" she whispers.

"Yeah, I heard them."

"So why aren't you looking?"

I look in her eyes, and it becomes clear. "I don't need to." I smile. She looks confused. "It's magic." *Just like you.*

# Christmas Day

## 2 YEARS LATER

"**B**abe?" I whisper, hoping it's enough to rouse Niamh. "Sweetheart?"

"No," she grumbles into her pillow.

I hold in my snicker because it pisses her off that I'm such a morning person. Usually, to counteract her unwillingness to open her eyes before 9 a.m. I wake her with my tongue caressing a certain area of her body. Today, however, I can't disregard the real possibility that Liam will come barging in. So, I'm having to wake her up in a way that's not satisfying to either of us.

"Honey, wake up. It's time." Instead of answering, she shoves a pillow over her head. "Ugh, Niamh, please don't make me get Liam."

She then bats me over the head with the pillow. So far, this is a wonderful Christmas morning. "I'm up," she says, rising from the bed like a bloody corpse.

Her hair is sticking out in several directions, and her sleep shirt is dropping off one shoulder. Smiling at the woman I'm totally in love with, I shuffle forward and run my hands through her bobbed hair. I always thought Niamh's long, lavish black hair was gorgeous. When she showed up one evening with her new style, I think I ravished her for five hours straight. That's how sexy she looked with shorter hair. Anyway, back to today, and the way she looks adorable when sleepy.

"I love you," I whisper into her mouth.

"I've got morning breath," she grumbles, but smiles when I deepen the kiss.

"I love it. Now, are you ready for your present?"

Niamh nips my nose. "I thought we weren't doing that, with your family so close by?"

"I didn't mean *that*. Get your head out of the gutter!"

"Well, Santa really shit the bed then, because I specifically asked for several orga—"

"Are you awake?" Liam's less-than-quiet voice rumbles through the door.

Niamh laughs, pulling me in for a quick kiss. "We're just getting up, buddy," she calls.

"Hurry up. We need to see if Santa's been!"

"Yeah, Niamh, hurry up," I mock. That earns me another pillow to the face. It looks like I'm going to have to wait to give Niamh her present. I wanted to do it when we were alone so we could have some time to celebrate without the family getting involved.

In the hallway, there's a line of adults all looking knackered. Liam is at the back because out of us Robinsons, he's always the one that wakes up earlier than the rest, and as a result has to be the last to go downstairs.

We watch Dad trundle down to the living room. We wait for the inevitable, "He's not been, let's go back to bed" before we all descend. Liam holds on until the last step and then body checks us all out of the way until he's by the Christmas tree, smiling giddily at the presents.

Mum makes hot chocolate for everyone, and I turn the oven on for the croissants. Niamh stays with Liam, Beth, and Dad. Ted takes Reggie outside.

The second Liam gets the go-ahead, he starts ripping into his presents. The rest of us take our time eating, drinking, and watching each other's reactions.

Mum's happy with her new scarf, spa package, and earrings. Beth is already crying, which is the norm nowadays. She has exceeded her due date by several days and is wildly irritated, causing her to either cry or shout. Ted is dealing with his wife by walking my dog. A lot. Tammy will be over later with little Pippa, and will become the Beth whisperer, which the rest of us Robinsons will greatly appreciate. Liam is already hooking up his new gaming console, so that will be him occupied for the next year. Dad is playing with a new tool of some sort. He did try to explain what it was for, but lost us all five minutes in. All I know is that it will help him make ukuleles.

"So?" Niamh says in my ear.

"I wanted to give you your present when we're alone," I whisper back.

"But you said it wasn't that kind of present," she replies, wiggling her eyebrows.

I laugh. "It's not. Ugh, okay, fine, here." I hand Niamh a slim package. She opens it gently but looks confused when she holds the key up.

"Um, babe… I have a key to your place." She does indeed. In fact, I gave it to her mere minutes after I moved into my houseboat.

"I know. This is a key to our place," I say nervously.

"What do you mean?"

I clear my throat and hope she's going to be happy. "I…I, um, rented that cottage you saw. The one with the vegetable garden."

"What do… What?"

"This is why I wanted to do this alone," I begin. "In case this isn't what you want."

"I don't know what I want, because I'm not sure what you're asking." Her eyes tell me she does know what I'm asking but needs me to verbalise it.

"I want to live with you. In our own house. I…I spoke to the landlord, and he's willing to give us a year's lease before putting it up for sale, with us having first refusal." It took me a lot of time to get Paul the landlord to enter into this agreement. I couldn't in good conscience up and buy a bloody house without Niamh's input, so this was the next best thing. He is expecting us to buy the place next year, and if I'm honest, I am too. Things with Niamh have been wonderful. We practically live together now, but it's not formal. Plus, I really want to live in a house that isn't on water.

"You... Us," she splutters.

"Yes, please," I reply against her lips.

"Yes. Oh my god, of course."

"What's happening over here?" Mum asks.

"Nic finally asked me to move in with her," Niamh shouts, flinging herself at me.

"Jesus, Nic. What the hell took you so long?" Beth grouses.

"Hey, it's a big decision. I wanted to make sure we were in the right place."

"You've been together for two years, sis."

"Beth—"

"It doesn't matter." Niamh laughs, cupping my face. "I'd have waited forever. I just wanted you to feel ready," she adds quieter. Out of the two of us, it's been me that has needed more time with changes in our relationship.

"I'm ready. I have been for a while and I would have asked sooner. It just took me a while to negotiate this deal with Paul." I go ahead and tell her everything Paul and I discussed.

"So, after the year, we could put in an offer to buy?"

"Yup." That earns me another tackle, which I love. "And then..." I say, because this next part is even more nerve-racking. "I thought we could..." I leave my sentence hanging and reveal the small ring box that I've hidden deep down in my elf onesie pocket. I didn't realise the rest of the room had grown silent. It's only when Liam gasps that I know we have everyone's attention. But my focus is solely on Niamh.

"Nicole," she gasps, her eyes on the box. I place it on her knee. After several silent moments, she opens it and covers her mouth with a hand. It's not the most expensive ring. But when I saw it, I knew it belonged on Niamh's finger. A simple white gold band with an emerald stone the same colour as her eyes.

"Niamh O'Conner, when you're ready to take that step. Will you marry me?"

"Yeah, she will," Liam shouts.

"Liam," Dad chastises. "Not now, mate."

"Yes, Nic. When *we're* ready, I absolutely will marry you."

With shaking hands, I pluck the ring out and slip it on her finger. Then I think we both forget there are others in the room because the kiss we start turns fiery, really quickly.

"Whoa, alright, reel it in, there are kids present," Aileen barks from the living room door. She and Wally always come over in the morning. Niamh and I pull apart, slightly out of breath and with matching wide smiles on our faces.

"Nim's going to be my proper sister," Liam announces, causing us to laugh.

"What did we miss?" Aileen asks.

"Nic finally pulled her finger out of her backside and asked Nim to move in and then marry her."

"Babe," Ted says softly. "Um, you're being a bit harsh." The glare he receives is hilarious. I'm sure his balls just jumped right back inside his body.

"Oh, I'm so happy," Aileen cries, sweeping in and taking us both in her arms. We spend the next few minutes hugging the family. Beth bursts out with loud, ugly tears, making the majority of us scatter. Champagne is needed.

Before we head back to Niamh's for the night, Beth

summons Liam and me to the War Room. How the hell she made it down the stairs is a mystery. She's as wide as the staircase.

"Beth, we could have met upstairs. No need to come down here."

She shakes her head. "It's tradition. The baby needs to understand that from an early age."

"Righto, so what's up?"

"Well, we've failed again."

Beth's right. We came no closer this year to finding the bells. The thing is, every time I hear them now, my first instinct is to kiss Niamh. My focus has changed. Two years ago, my life changed and the magic of the bells helped, I'm sure of it. So, I don't really want to find the truth anymore.

"Maybe it's time we accepted defeat?"

"You don't want to look for the bells anymore?"

Oh shit, I think she's about to cry again. "No, of course I do! Um…"

"No, I think you might be right." She sighs. "Plus, I want to make sure this little one and Pippa get the same experience we got over Christmas. I don't suppose I can be running around looking for sleigh bells while trying to teach her about the magic of Christmas."

Liam sits next to Beth, stroking his beard. It's thick and well-groomed. Niamh bought him a beard kit for his birthday and I have to say, the man looks good. He's a big, loveable dork in his Superman t-shirt and snowman sleep trousers. "I don't mind if we stop looking."

Beth and I look at him curiously. "Really? But what about proving Mum works for Santa?"

"I already know she does. I just wanted to spend time with you two." Well, fuck, that's enough to start my tear ducts leaking. "But it's better now you both live here. And I know we can't spend all of December together now because of work and stuff, but that's okay. I get to come 'round your houses and see you all the time. So, I don't mind if we stop Operation Sleigh Bells."

I run a hand through my hair. "Wow, so that's it. We're just stopping?"

"Or we come up with our own way to make Christmas awesome for the next generation of Robinsons," Beth suggests, shrugging her shoulders.

"That sounds fun." Liam smiles. "Can we talk about it tomorrow, though? I need to have a bath and go to bed."

"Sure thing, buddy. See you tomorrow."

We watch Liam run up the stairs.

"He's doing really well," I say.

After Beth told me about Liam's need to feel more included with the adults, we sat down as a family and had a chat. Liam will always have limitations, but he doesn't need us to treat him with kiddie gloves. In the two years since the meeting, Liam has been learning new things, and taking on more responsibility. He even works at The Soggy Biscuit part-time. Funnily enough, it helped curb his appetite for scones.

"I think we're all doing better," Beth replies. "I'm proud of you, Nic, for coming home and making a life with Niamh. I'm sure happy to have you around."

"Really, because all you've done is shout at me for the past six months." I laugh.

"Baby rage." She grins.

"I'm happy to be home, too. Speaking of my lovely lady. I need to get back upstairs. Can I give you a hand?"

"Nic, you're gonna need more than a hand. Call Ted. This is going to need some muscle."

"In that case, I should fetch Tammy."

Beth looks at me. "Good point."

Once Beth is safely upstairs, I find Niamh, and we head out. It still feels strange not sleeping in my old room every night over Christmas, but I wouldn't change it. I may be months away from my forties now, but the magic this time of year elicits is still as strong as ever. Maybe more so now I have Niamh by my side. She doesn't know it, but engraved on the inside of her engagement ring is a tiny sleigh bell. A little reminder that those bells have brought me more love and happiness than I could ever imagine.

And who knows, maybe one day it will be our kids who hear them and discover the meaning behind the delicate jingles. And maybe one of those kids could finally stop Reggie from losing his shit every time a doorbell chimes. Now, that would be a Christmas miracle.

The End

# Thank you!

Thank you for reading Waiting for Eternity.
**Spill the Tea (in a Review)!**
If this book gave you butterflies, made you swoon, or
kept you up way past your bedtime, I'd love to hear
about it! Reviews help indie authors like me reach more
readers who are searching for their next sapphic romance
obsession. Drop a review on Amazon, Goodreads, or
wherever you love to share your bookish thoughts. Even
a quick "loved it!" makes a huge difference.

You're the best!

# Stay Connected

### Don't Miss Out!

Love steamy sapphic romance? Join my newsletter for new release alerts, promotions, book recommendations, and special reader-only perks. Sign up now: https://alysonroot.com/

### <u>Become a VIP Member</u>

Want the ultimate insider experience? My VIP membership gives you early access to new books, exclusive bonus content, behind-the-scenes insights, member discounts, and a front-row seat to my creative process. Plus, you'll be part of a community of readers who love these stories as much as I love writing them. Join the VIP club:

VIP MEMBERSHIP

# Let's Talk About Pleasure

I write characters who own their desires, communicate openly, and prioritise their pleasure—because that's how it should be in real life, too.

As a sex-positive author, I'm all about breaking down stigma and celebrating what feels good. That's why I'm thrilled to partner with *Wet For Her*, a queer-run online adult toy store that's as inclusive and empowering as the stories I write.

I use their products myself, and I can vouch for their quality, care, and commitment to the community. Ready to explore and get 10% off your purchase? Visit them through my affiliate link:

Web link: Toys

or

Checkout Code: ALYSONROOT

Your pleasure matters!

**Transparency Corner**: Yep, this is an affiliate link. If you make a purchase, I get a little kickback. Think of it as buying me a metaphorical coffee while exploring some fun products. Win-win!

# Other Titles By Alyson Root

A Dance Towards Forever

Diving Into Her

Always Emilie

Broken Parts Included

Love & Other Wild Things

Finding Molly Parsons

Keeping Carmen Ruiz

The Wisdom of Bug

Sleigh Bells Ring

Risking Immortality

Waiting for Eternity

Fighting for Infinity

Mob's Seduction

Playing Her Heart

Welcome to Ero-TEA-Ca: We're Open!

Once Upon a Time in December

# About the author

Alyson was born and raised in the heart of England. She moved to Paris in 2015 when she met her wife. Together they moved to the west of France, where they now live with their two dogs. Alyson spends her time reading sapphic fiction books, writing and Scuba Diving.

Alyson discovered her love of writing in her mid-thirties. Her debut book, *A Dance Towards Forever*, was inspired by her wife and their very own love story. Alyson wrote *Diving Into Her* and award-winning *Always Emilie*, which added with her first book, created The French Connection series.

www.alysonroot.com
a.rootauthor@alysonroot.com

HUMAN AUTHORED™

THE
AG Authors Guild®

7683247